Anna Begins

Anna Begins

Jennifer Davenport

Black Heron Press
P.O. Box 13396
Mill Creek, Washington 98082
www.blackheronpress.com

Copyright © 2008 Jennifer Davenport. All rights reserved.

Jacket art and design by Sarah Sandman

ISBN 978-0-930773-83-0

Black Heron Press
Post Office Box 13396
Mill Creek, Washington 98082
www.blackheronpress.com

Contents

Anna Begins

Her kindness bangs a gong
It's moving me along
And Anna begins to fade away
She's chasing me away
She disappears and
Oh Lord, I'm not ready for this sort of thing
—Adam Duritz (Counting Crows), "Anna Begins"

PROLOGUE

U2.

I haven't heard this song in *forever*. Ain't love the sweetest thing.

I had to get out. I hate lying.

"What's this?" She asked when she picked up my box of Correctol.

I'd just gone grocery shopping and picked up a case of Strawberry Ultra SlimFast for her. My mother is a size five. I'm allowed an indulgence too.

I didn't pause. "Laxatives."

She looked at me blankly. I smiled. Then I did the confidential best friend thing. I leaned in.

"Problems." I said this quietly. When I was younger, I used to get sick a lot. She nodded and smiled. She seemed almost comfortable with the illusion that things hadn't changed. She walked back into the kitchen. Have another shake, Ma.

But now I have to pick up Em at Church.

Church. I'm not sure what I think about that. I don't doubt there is a God or anything. I just doubt myself.

I write. Mostly poetry.

A lot of it is about wanting to be young again.

I want to be five again.

Before I knew what fat was. Before I knew what a year was. Before I knew what sex was. And I want to stay there because I was innocent and smart and pretty.

I want only to feel guilt for things outside myself. I want to feel guilt for breaking dishes and losing my sister's blue elephant. I don't want that guilt where the only person who is disappointed in myself is me.

Does Jeremy feel that guilt? Does Lauren? Does my mother? How about Katie? Do they ever get that sick feeling in the pit of their stomachs when they think about themselves? Do they ever regret themselves?

I can't suppose that Katie does. Maybe she feels regret for me. Maybe she regrets Jeremy—or Lauren. But I don't think she regrets herself.

I think only because I've stopped knowing about Katie.

I could call her my best friend. Or maybe I wouldn't call her anything at all - it's been two months since any calling has taken place. Our last conversation: November at Wendy's.

"We haven't gone out in so long." I said this while I was playing with a plate of nacho salad.

"Oh, I know. Well, I've been really busy with stuff, you know?"

Stuff.

"Yeah. "

Stuff happened to her. Stuff kept happening. And so, we had to stop being so she could continue to have stuff happen. What do you do when you have no one to talk things over with? I write.

I can see Emily's breath when she leans in the passenger side "You're late. Mom didn't want to pick me up?"
"No. She forgot and then asked me to do it for her. She's busy. Talking to someone on the phone."
"Mike?"
Mike. Or maybe Jim. I shrug. "Maybe. I didn't ask."
Boyfriends.
This is what boyfriends remind me of:
Mommy closes the door. There is a party outside.
"Don't tell Tom what I'm doing, Lissy."
I look at her and she strips. In my bedroom. With people outside. Tom is out there too. Tom is nice.
"What's that?"
It's a garter belt. I have no idea what purpose it serves. I think it's white. She puts her clothing back on over this complicated contraption.
Shhh. Don't tell Tom, Lissy. It's a surprise for him.
I don't understand. Someday I will. But for now, I'm five.

JEREMY

He spent the drive home alternating his hand with mine between his legs. My hand at stop lights, and his the rest of the drive. Twice after a green, he gently placed my hand back between my own legs and told me softly to keep busy. We needed a place to park.
I told him we'd use my father's driveway. What the

heck. We'd just been at Dave's house doing the same thing under a pink blanket in a small room populated by five other people. Katie was on the couch right next to him—his head on her shoulder. His ex and my best friend. Either way, we still needed a place to park.

I suppose details aren't necessary. In my mind, it all happened at once—he put his car in park, I lifted my dress. His right hand immediately on my left breast and his left hand between my legs. His tongue in my mouth, my tongue in his, and my left hand groping for his crotch—an area of his anatomy I'd only just become familiar with under that pink blanket. He fingered me, I jerked him off, then I tucked myself back into my dress and ran up the icy driveway to get him a pen so I could write out directions for him to get home.

I came back to his car and he looked sick.

I was cold and forgot how to draw a map.

I ended up getting in my car and leading him back to a main road.

I hate every word I just wrote.

I'm seventeen and my name is Melissa.

Less than nineteen hours later, I find myself listening to my mother give me the birth control talk.

"You're going to college next year," She says, "And you're going to get involved with people sexually."

I nod. I smile. Thanks mom. Thanks.

For seventeen years, sex in college, let alone sex with anyone at all in the near future was a foreign idea to me.

That was two weeks ago. Between now and then, Jeremy happened.

I'm best friends with Katie. He's best friends with Katie, too. *We* might even be called best friends. But only since he and Katie broke up. We're secret. We're sly. We're amazing. We're horny. We're fuck-buddies without the fuck and until tonight, without anything but kissing.

I was kind of in a daze when he took my hand from between my legs and brought it over between his legs. I can tell you exactly what went through my head when I realized what it was I was touching. No fireworks or anything like I thought there'd be. Just the thought:

"Hard...dick..."

I swear to God.

ERIC

At around two AM, I get out of my car and slide up the icy driveway slowly in five-inch platforms, wondering why I hadn't taken them off before. I don't notice until later that the back of my dress is still partially unzipped. It is fifteen degrees with windchill and I am wearing a semi-formal dress with no jacket. I barely notice the extra draft. Stumbling inside, I grab a croissant from the kitchen counter and shiver as I walk upstairs. The light is on in the TV room. I peek in and Eric is sitting on the floor in front of the TV, his back against the end of the lounge.

I walk into the room, attempting to maintain an air of

situational and emotional control: "Do you know what
time it is?"

"I was hoping you could tell me."

He is nineteen. He is my step-brother. He has been a
god since I was twelve. "Nope. It was one-thirty when I
left Dave's—but that was a long time ago."

One finger-fuck ago.

"Oh. I bought a new game."

"Really?"

"Yeah. *Gran Tourismo*. Car racing. Wanna race me?"

"Yeah. I just wanna get some dinner."

I have finished the croissant already.

"You haven't had any?"

"Of course not." I fluff my wrinkled dress. "Never eat
before or during a dance. It's a girl thing."

He laughs. "That's stupid."

Watching him laugh makes me smile. "I know."

I change quickly in my room. Addidas pants, bra,
T-shirt, socks. With the dress, shoes and shaper gone, I
down two Correctol tablets and run downstairs to micro-
wave a slice of pizza. I grab another croissant and run
back upstairs to lie down at the end of the lounge, my
head an inch or so from his. I'm starving.

"Did you hear me run in fifteen minutes ago?"

"No. Didn't you just get home?"

He hadn't noticed us in the driveway. I was relieved
and now almost wanted to tell him. Almost.

"Yeah. But I had to lead Jeremy home, so I was in for a
second about fifteen minutes ago for my keys."

"You had to lead him home?"

"He wasn't feeling well and I couldn't give coherent directions."

He pauses the game and turns to study me for a second. "You look tired."

"I am."

"You okay? How was the dance?"

"Less gay than I thought it would be. But my friends are boring."

"Oh?" He smiles. The heavens shine.

"They all sat around after the dance. We didn't do anything exciting. *Austin Powers* out-takes." I sigh dramatically and continue briefly, "Not even the actual movie—just the out-takes."

He nods. "After I finish this race, you want to race me?"

I smile. "I'd be honored." He un-pauses and goes back to playing.

I eat a little and then stare at the back of his neck.

Someday, I hope.

Then I put my pizza down, suddenly tasting Jeremy back in my mouth.

I console myself. At least I'll have had experience.

He turns his head slightly and my eyes droop watching the muscles in his neck change their position. Everything suddenly begins to happen in slow motion. He smiles softly and I watch in awe at the turning up of his mouth. From far away, he says something that takes me a minute to understand.

"If you were bored, I would have gone to pick you up, you know."

I smile and nod. My eyes droop again and the world disappears into the pillow at the end of the lounge.

MOM

"You're getting so skinny!" My mother smiles proudly.

"Thanks. "

"So," She says in a confidential best-friends manner, "what's your secret?"

Laxatives.

"Nothing. Guess I'm just eating less."

The smile widens, "Pretty soon, there will be nothing left!" Joking laugh. Great. My mother actually loves me now that I'm an anorexic.

You know that whole social concept about weight not mattering and how it's the person inside that counts? Bullshit. If you're thin, the world loves you. And I hate it. I talk my way out of taking the compliment.

"Maybe it's just the pants. They're flares. In think they're supposed to make you look thinner."

Disappointed look followed by a recovery smile. "No, I really think you're losing a *bunch* of weight."

Yup. Lemme go take another Correctol.

"Well, I gotta go work on my report now." I hold up a bunch of books, the top one titled *Gay Rights* in big white letters. There are two guys on the cover sitting in a cafe.

"Wait. Before you go," She pauses to see if I care.

"Yeah?" It's not like my room is *that* far away. I turn my head and look longingly down the hall at it. She takes the point, but keeps going.

"Are you and Jeremy...*dating*?" The word sounds dirty.

"*No.*" I turn to go.

"Because it seems to me that..."

"I mean, he's *Jeremy*. Of course not. If you were in high school, would *you* date Jeremy?"

Please shut up, please shut up. She doesn't.

"Yes. He's a very nice boy. I wish I had met some nice boys like him when *I* was in high school."

You mean when you were fat. I know what you mean. I'm fat. I meet a nice boy. Hang on to him. Whatever.

"Whatever." I turn once more, showing her a flash of the back of HOMOSEXUALITY: *Lesbians, Gays and You*, and start down the hall. But she just can't let me go.

"Melissa. "

Grrr.

"What?"

"Do you have, maybe, eight minutes?"

"No. I only have seven. I'll talk later."

She winces, but chooses not to pounce at my comment.

"Seven is fine. We should have a talk."

I stay standing where I had stopped. She looks at me.

"I really have to do this report." *Gay Rights* makes another appearance from under my arm to emphasize my point. She ignores my pleas and walks past me into the living room. She sits and pats the cushion next to her, her hand asking me to take a seat.

"Come on, it'll just take a second."

"I don't have a second."

"Yes you do. Come on, sweetie."

I sit on an ottoman across the room from her.

"What?"

"Can't you sit next to me? What happened to my sweet Lissy who liked talking to her mommy?"

"She was five. She was young. She was stupid."

"Lis. Sit down next to me."

I don't want an argument over seats. I drag my feet and sit down next to her with the most possible noise.

"What?"

"Well, when I was your age, my mother never talked to me about anything. I had to learn about it all on my own. Of course, you can get hurt very easily by learning things on your own, so I thought I'd help you out by talking to you about things you may not know very much about—especially in the world outside of health class."

Very sneaky. It's a sex talk. I try to avoid it.

"Mom. I know how to put a Tampon in. In fact, I have one in right now. I'm fine. I swear." PMS. Sarcasm. Can't she tell I'm not worth it?

"You're going to college next year," she says sweetly, "and you're going to get involved with people sexually."

I nod. I smile. Thanks, mom. Thanks.

LAUREN

History.

"I'd like all the boys on this side of the room to be the Supreme Court." He motions to split the room in half. The males on my half of the room get up and move their desks to the front and haphazardly form Mr. Keyes' imaginary Supreme Court. The rest of the class is left as audience. I immediately get up and move a seat back to sit near Katie and Lauren. Jeremy, who had been sitting next to me, is already up front.

"Lauren." I whisper loudly at her. She turns to look at me.

She smiles and whispers back, "I have to tell you something. I have *issues*."

I look at her. I raise my eyebrows.

Rich?

She nods.

Yeah.

I smile, then turn serious again, "I have something to tell you too."

Now it's her turn to raise her eyebrows and she does so knowingly. But I can't read her expression.

I smile, feeling clueless. "What?"

"How was Saturday?"

"Fine. That's what I have to tell you about."

She raises her eyebrows again. Same reaction. She knows.

"What? You and Jeremy?"

Yes, but how did she...

"*No.*"

"Oh. Tell me later."

"You too."

Katie turns to look at us.

"What's up?"

We look at each other.

"Nothing."

"Nothing."

Jinx. We smile sweetly.

"So, Katie," Lauren says, attempting a very smooth save, "How *was* Saturday?"

"Boring. Afterwards, we went to Dave's house and watched *Austin Powers* out-takes. I fell asleep." She shrugs and turns back.

I sigh. She hadn't noticed us on the couch. Amazing as it is. Then I hear Lauren whisper at the back of my head.

"You two hooked up."

Yes.

No.

"*No.*"

I suppose it doesn't matter if she knows. She's out of our "group." Now if Katie were to find out, *that* would be against the rules.

I give her one more look before turning back around.

Yes.

EMILY

Male voice.

"Is Emily there?"

"Hold on." I say this in my most monotonous of voices. It's Chris. I bring the phone into Emily's room. "Em, for you." I hold the phone out like a dead animal. She smiles and grabs it, greeting the male voice.

"Hello? Oh!" She smiles brightly. "It's you!" Yep, it's him. Get over it. You've got a sign taped to your mirror that clearly states: *Don't date Chris.* Follow your own advice and get off the phone with the asshole. She is fifteen.

I shuffle back into the kitchen. My mom looks up from her paperwork.

"Chris?" She looks at me. I nod.

"Yup."

She frowns and I sit back down to finish my soup. She doesn't approve. I smirk at my bowl and she sees it. I know and so does she. Her boyfriends were never any better. She can't blame us for making bad choices.

I look at her. She glares. Yeah, she knows it. I lean back over my bowl and return to revising my report.

I barely notice when she gets up and retrieves the school phone directory and the *Bell Atlantic Users Guide* from the counter across the kitchen. "Christophe—not very Greek, is it?" I look up and see her looking at the phone directory. I look down at it. *Tsilas, Christophe.*

"Mom, I think the directory only had room for the letters up to E. It's Christopher. "

"Oh." She runs her finger across the line to his telephone number and then opens her *Bell Atlantic Users Guide*. What is she...suddenly, it clicks.

"You're not—"

"Don't tell her."

"I won't tell her. But she's gonna figure it out."

"I don't care. She won't know how to undo it."

"All right. Whatever works." I walk out of the kitchen to staple my report.

She calls after me. "You can tape signs to your mirror all you want, but in the end you're gonna do what you want anyway. Someone needs to intervene."

Emily is depressed. She has been since they broke up. Does mom know she cuts? Maybe she has only once. A year in counseling and she still talks to him on the phone every day. I probably would have blocked his number myself if my mom hadn't already taken the initiative.

I walk by Emily's room again and I hear her laugh. Gay Rights. Think Gay Rights.

I stop myself from going into her room.

JEREMY

School parking lot. He makes a joke. "I'm sure Saturday made up for that though." He laughs. I look at him. It's Tuesday.

"Uh, yeah." I am beyond unamused.

"Oh, right. We should talk about that." We haven't made mention of it since it happened.

I hate being the girl. "Yeah, we probably should." I look at him carefully. It's the same friendly face that I have met every time I look. He looks right back at me. I put the car in park.

"So," He waits. I look out the windshield and think for a moment.

"You looked sick when I came back to write you directions."

"I was just tired. It was catching up with me. Nothing to do with you."

"Okay, just making sure."

"What did you think?"

I hadn't really thought about what I thought, so I pause to think.

"You know when something happens to you, and when you think about it later, you can't believe it really happened to you, so you keep rewinding it in your memory?" I realize this statement sounds ditzy.

"So it was positive?"

I guess. I can't say no.

"Yeah."

He nods. "I liked it too." Pause. "But I kinda had mixed feelings about some things."

Mixed is a kind word.

"Katie was on the couch."

"Yeah. Like that."

We sit in agreement for a moment.

I suddenly want to suggest an idea. "Although, the idea of getting away with that in a room full of people is kind of a turn-on."

He looks at me and almost cracks a smile as his hand slips between my legs. "Yeah, that too."

I look at him. What are we doing? Again, that friendly face. I can never read it. I'm wearing gloves, so I hold off on making any sort of move. I try to keep talking.

"I was tired too, when I got in. I changed and went in to watch TV with Eric."

"Did he notice?"

Did he notice what? Behavior? I think, trying to ignore the hand. Oh, yes, that.

"No, I asked him if he had heard me come in to get my keys. He hadn't. He was playing a video game. He was oblivious. No one saw us out there." I'm sick and embarrassed that I chose the driveway. I want to take that decision back. I want to say more. I'm panicking. I'm being awkward. I want to leave my skin.

The friendly face only looks relieved and the hand is all the way up my inner thigh.

The student lot is empty.

"I wrote something about it. Did you want to read it?"

He smiles. "You wrote something about it?"

"Yeah. It's what I do. I write. It's what I have to do. It's not finished yet. I hope you don't mind."

"No." He smiles. "Do I get part of the profits when it's published?"

"How about just the satisfaction of making enough of an impact on my life for me to want to include you in a story."

He smiles. "Point zero one percent of the profits?"

I laugh. "Okay, fine. Just don't tell any of the other characters."

He nods and smiles. "Deal." I reach into the back seat, grab it out of my bag, and hold it for a second, looking at it. I can't believe I wrote this. I rationalized that Toni Morrison and a lot of other great women writers have more explicit things in their books. I'll be fine. Why do I feel sick?

"It can't be that bad..." He tries to look over my shoulder at it. Nervously, I hand it to him. He takes it and it's no longer just mine. He begins reading and his hand moves to my crotch.

"In the story, your character's name is Jeremy," I say this weakly. I lean over to read my own words, which now look so foreign to me.

He spent the drive home alternating his hand with mine between his legs...

I slowly take my gloves off. I rest my head gently on his shoulder and let it happen again.

MOM

I hang my gym pants on the back of my kitchen chair. They still smell like me.

"Little surprises are nice, aren't they?" It's dark in the kitchen and my mother is cleaning the stove. I hadn't realized how old she has gotten until right now. She used to be the most beautiful person in the world.

"Yeah." I'm running my hands along my gym pants because I had forgotten how nice they feel.

"You should have invited Katie in, you know."

"She had to get home and do homework. She has other stuff to do."

Stuff.

"Oh, right. And you wanted to go to bed."

"Yeah. But it was nice of her to stop over for a sec." She came to return my gym pants.

"Little surprises *are* nice."

"They are."

She re-folds the dishcloth. "If we take Emily's friends skiing on Saturday, you may have to drive up behind us. We need your car to put the skis in."

"That's fine." Everything is experience.

"Or I could ask Mike to come and you could ride up with him." That works too. "You like Mike, right?" Yeah, I do. I nod. Like Mike. Drink Gatorade.

She's always asking me if I like him cos she knows I do. Right now, they are "just friends." I like Mike enough to hope that he avoids becoming a boyfriend.

"Whatever works out best for everyone." I say this. Truthfully, my mind's made up. Driving up with Mike would be fun.

I wander out of the kitchen and into the basement. I

put some wet clothing into the dryer and walk back up into the dark kitchen. I almost walk out, but stop by the TV. There's a pile of my mom's mail on the counter.

Dear Insured: Our Plan Administrator has recently completed an audit of your Financial Institution's Accidental Death and Dismemberment Insurance Plan.

Death and Dismemberment. I picture an unsuspecting office employee being decapitated by a pencil sharpener gone haywire. What a fun thing to get in the mail. I can't wait until I'm old so I can get mail like this. I want to say something witty about the letter, but she says something first.

"I called a couple of times this afternoon—no one picked up and the phone kept on ringing."

I knew it was you. I ignored the Call Waiting.

"I'm sorry. The phone got left off the hook." All wit killed, I turn away from the stack of mail to look at her. The dishcloth she is wiping the stove with is faded. It used to be blue.

"I really wanted to get through." You always want to get through. Can't leave us alone.

"Yeah." I want to go out the door and return to my bedroom, but I keep watching her.

"You know the reason I wanted to get through…" She starts her statement and then stops it to wipe the handle of the coffee pot. None of us drink coffee and I don't want to know her reason for wanting to get through. Mike drinks coffee. I wait for her to finish.

"The reason I wanted to get through was because I

wanted to tell you how much I'm going to miss you in the next year."

And how much you feel like you've missed us growing up.

"And how I really feel like I missed out on you growing up."

The reason I waited so long to have kids was so I could stay home and take care of them.

"The reason I waited so long to have my babies was so I could stay home with them and take care of them."

And now you're going away and I haven't been able to do that.

"And you're going to college in the fall and I've never had a chance to do that with you."

I just wish things could have been different.

"I don't think you know how much I wish that things could have been different."

And how much I wish your father hadn't taken that away from me.

She says nothing.

Bastard.

She puts the dishcloth under the faucet and wets it again. It bothers me that it's so faded.

"Yeah." I say softly. "I know." I walk out of the room and don't wait for her to blame him.

JEREMY

"Yeah, something did bother me."

Monday evening. My house. I wait for him to continue.

"Do you really think you need to take laxatives?"

Why does everyone pick on the laxatives?

I raise my eyebrows and look at him.

"You don't have to tell me if you don't want to."

I don't. But I do it anyway.

"I do it because starvation, bulimia and caffeine pills didn't work." There. It's out.

"You mean you've tried other methods?"

I nod. "My mom has had me on diets since I was nine. It's kind of ingrained in my nature. I'm ugly." I shrug. I'm serious.

"No," He suddenly looks frustrated. "Lis, I would never kiss an ugly girl. I don't think I could do it." He's serious too.

"I guess I know I'm not. I just feel that way." I try to smile.

Contradictions. I wasn't fishing for compliments.

I wonder why I'm subjecting myself to this. No secrets for Melissa. I want to go back to Sunday and ignore the impulse to write.

I sigh and focus the conversation. His opinion is most important. "I was really just asking about the parts with you in it. Did any of that upset you?"

"Oh. No, I think it's pretty accurate...of course, there's a lot more to me."

"I know. Well, there's more to me too. But I'm not going to write any more details about our..." I pause, not wanting to say *thing*, "...relationship."

He nods again. He seems relieved. I continue.

"It's not necessary. I just needed it for the beginning."

His expression changes and he laughs. "You mean you used me?" I laugh too.

"God, no. That's why I'm not writing about it anymore."

In some ways, I regret having let him read it. I don't want to hurt his feelings by showing him only parts of my own.

"I suppose I'd have to read it again. I didn't really pay attention the first time."

He says this with a smile and I smile too.

"Understandable." At least it seems we're comfortable with the *thing* now.

With that, there is nothing more to say and I look at him. He says nothing. We lean in and kiss. Then something brings us back apart and he gets up from the bed.

"I guess I can't just hang out at Melissa's anymore." He wanders a few feet away to look at a picture frame.

Something twinges in my heart. I suddenly want to take it all back. I feel briefly panicked.

"Well, maybe we could stop?" It's a pointless suggestion. I'm suddenly confused as to why I've even said it.

He looks up from the picture and over at me. "I don't think so."

"I don't want this to keep us from hanging out, though. I like being around you."

He walks back over to me. "Lis! We're best friends!
The thing is just a thing."
I smile weakly. "Yeah, I know. I just...got worried.
Sorry."
He laughs.

LAUREN

I am drama queen. Lauren isn't listening.
"I think I'm getting an ulcer."
"Lis, I can't put this down."
"My life—the marking period ended, you know. I'm
going to die."
"This is *really* good."
I stop and look at her.
"What?"
She stops too and nods slightly, waving the sheets of
white. "This."
I look at her. "The story?"
"Yeah. Is this real? I know it is."
"Parts of it." I lie. "I take parts of my life and add it to
fiction."
"Yeah, I noticed. I mean, Dad's girlfriend's son? Come
on, you put him in everything."
I smile. "He's a good topic. He's allowed. Plus, this
time I'm keeping it real."
She laughs. "Whatever. Who's Jeremy?"
"No one." It's 8:30 on Monday night. Two hours ago,

No one was on my bed. Now Lauren is.

"Oh, come on! Who is he?" She nudges me.

I look at her, half cracking a smile. I can't believe she didn't figure it out. Maybe she's in denial. She doesn't really need to know who he is. He's no one.

"No one!" I say this with a smile. "He's the fiction part. This didn't really happen. I got the name from the Pearl Jam song." She loves Pearl Jam.

"Okay, okay!" She drops it and goes on. "Lauren and Katie—who are they?"

"The names I got from two girls where I work. Lauren and Katie. I like Lauren. I—" I think Katie is a bitch. But I pick my words carefully. "I tend to get annoyed by Katie."

She smiles. I add, "You're Lauren, actually. Her character." I hold my hands out as if demonstrating the obvious. "You."

She smiles. "Oh, and Katie—they were doing it on the *couch*. That's so bad. You're so bad. That is *so* something that would actually happen."

I smile and smooth the comforter. I remind myself to be objective. It's not me. "I thought putting that in would make it pretty interesting. I tried to make it real."

Real. I look around. I smell him. I think it's my sweatshirt. Maybe I'm paranoid.

"It is, it is! It *so* is! I like, love this story. Can I have a copy?"

"Yeah, you can keep that one." I smell him when I'm in English class too. I must be paranoid. I hold my sleeve up to my nose and sniff it. It always smells like him. Even after I wash it.

"I want to show this to Meg. Is that okay? I'm always talking about you to her." She really likes it. I can tell. That makes me happy. Does she smell him? I must really be losing it. Maybe my mom changed detergents.

"Yeah, I'd be honored to have Meg read it. Please do." I smile.

Then I take my sweatshirt off.

JEREMY

English room. After school.

"I haven't looked at it for a week."

In story-land, a week is a long time. But even after a long time, sometimes, things don't change much. I ended up inviting Jeremy to go skiing. We drove up separately from my mom, Em and her friends. We skied. We drove home. We had fun. Nothing happened. Nor did I want it to.

"Maybe I need a new character."

"You could write about the restaurant on Saturday night."

"Yeah–character interaction. I thought that would be good, too. Jeremy and Lauren talking about the story. Problem is, nothing that you guys said was really that interesting. It was all like, 'Yeah, I like it, do you?', 'Yeah. It's good.'" Jeremy nods. "And anyway, it's Wednesday.

I was tired after skiing and I don't remember Saturday night that well."

"Make it up."

"Not when everything else is real."

"So now what?"

"Kim says I should create a lesbian character."

"*Are* you a lesbian?"

"No. But you'd like that, wouldn't you?"

Guys and lesbians. He shrugs and smiles. "Makes things interesting."

Interesting. "Maybe that's why Melissa was carrying the gay rights books."

Finding symbolism in my own life. Creepy.

He watches my expression with a smile on his face. "*Was* that the reason Melissa was carrying gay rights books?"

I laugh. "No. I just happened to be carrying gay rights books when it happened. "

"Oh." Mock disappointment. He smiles.

"I'll get you in on it if there's some lesbian action, I promise."

His smile widens. I laugh.

"Lauren says I need another guy. I don't want another guy though, unless it's Melissa's dad. Otherwise, she really will look like a slut. Which I'm not."

I even confuse myself sometimes.

"No. You're not." He nods thoughtfully. I continue.

"Problem with this method of writing is that if my life's not interesting, I can't write my story." I laugh. "I have to actually go out and do things now!"

He nods again.

"Although, I really can't, 'cause then it will all look planned and it's supposed to be slice-of-life." I stop. I'm blabbering. I'm boring myself.

"Oh, did I tell you? My dad thought I had a hangover Sunday morning."

Jeremy out drinking. With me. I laugh. It's a funny thought.

"Oh yeah. Out all night drinking with Lissa."

"He didn't know I was out with you. He just knew I didn't wake up until twelve-thirty! That, and my clothes smelled like smoke. I went to put them on this morning and I was like, what's that smell? I realized it was my pants."

"Well, it *was* a bar. What did you expect? Anyway, didn't your dad know you were skiing all day? One would assume you'd be tired."

"Probably. I don't know. Waking up at twelve-thirty isn't too unusual for me. My waking up at twelve-thirty in a daze with red, swollen eyes and smoky clothing is somewhat unusual. He always thinks I'm out drinking."

I think for a moment.

"I woke up with a hangover once."

The room is suddenly silent. I look around with a self-aware smile. English teacher acknowledges private conversation and I wait for her to ignore us again. I laugh slightly and white noise returns.

"As I was saying, yeah, I did it just once. Never

again."

He nods. "When was this?"

"With Jess. We were at a concert."

"How much did you drink?"

Does it matter?

"It doesn't really matter. Point is, waking up is nasty."

"No, I'd really like to know."

"I know you'd like to know."

"What, was it like, three or four?"

"It doesn't matter!" I know I'm not going to escape spilling. I prolong it anyway.

"But I want to know!"

"We were at a concert and Jess sees this older guy she thinks is hot. I'm not myself and I go up to him and ask him for a sip of his drink. He says fine. He buys us some. We both end up a little off."

Conspiratorial smile. "So how much?"

Numbers.

"Total?"

"Total."

I don't even remember.

"I don't remember." I say this with a smile. Mistake.

"Yes you do!"

Now I feel like I'd disappoint him if I don't. I estimate.

"Three. Plus, I had some sips from a few other guys'."

Upon reflection, little Date Rape Pill warning signs go off in my head.

"Whoa, Lis!"

"On top of that, my mom picked us up. We were sitting in the back seat looking at each other trying not to laugh. No one really knew about that 'cept Jess. Congrats for you. "

"Thanks. "

Twenty minutes later, I drive him to his car in the student lot.

"You look tired." I smile slightly.

"I am." He kisses the palm of his hand and taps my cheek lightly. "I should go home and sleep."

"Yeah." I agree.

He kisses the palm of his hand and taps my cheek again. I smile.

"Thanks. Now get home."

He unbuckles his seatbelt and sits there for a second. I watch him.

"Follow me home?"

I was going to anyway. He passed out in the middle of our conversation five minutes ago.

"Of course. If you swerve off the road and cause an accident, I'll be right behind you to paste myself to your bumper." I smile softly.

He nods. He kisses the palm of his hand and taps my cheek. I laugh.

"How many times are you going to do that?"

He shakes his head. "I should get home." He gets out of the car and shuts the passenger side door. He starts getting into his car and then walks back to my car and opens the door to the back seat.

"Forgot my bag."

He crawls across the backseat and grabs his bag from behind me. He stops on his crawl backwards to look at me. I smile and kiss him quickly and lightly. A friend kiss.

"Now get home. Go to sleep." *Take care of yourself. I care.*

He smiles. He leans through to the front seat. We kiss again. And again. My foot is still on the brake and my seatbelt is still on. A hand is down my shirt and I don't care.

"Maybe I'll just sleep here."

"If you want."

I'm not sure what I mean.

Nothing really changes. I decide not to write tonight.

THE GIRLS IN THE BATHROOM

Ninth-period statistics class.

Her blue eye shadow is bothering me. I decide to say something.

"You have pretty eyes."

Except for that goddamned eye shadow. It's cookie-monster blue. And she put it on *heavy.*

She smiles. "Thanks. They change color."

So do mine. But I'm not wearing ground Muppet.

"Yeah. Mine do that sometimes too. Depends on the

color I'm wearing."

She pulls at her magenta fleece vest.

"Pink usually makes mine look more blue."

What possessed you to buy a magenta fleece?

"Oh, I like that!" I say enthusiastically. "Where'd you buy it?" Like hell, I'm interested.

She smiles, happy someone approves of her trendy purchase.

"Old Navy. That's, like, my favorite store."

Oh, yay. They shouldn't allow you to purchase such a hideous garment. You're too ugly to pull it off.

Fake smile. Thanks for the advice. "Wow. Maybe I should take a look in there. I *never* go in there." For reasons now made especially obvious to me.

"Oh! You should! It's so cheap!" I can tell.

I smile amiably and look back down at my desk. She stays turned to face me. Don't you have some statistics to learn, woman? Turn around in your seat! But Ms. Daniels is too absorbed in her TI-83 to ask her to leave me alone.

"Oh my god, Lis, you have to hear this."

No, I don't. I lean in to listen like a good female. Gossip, baby.

"Kay. "

"You know how I left for the bathroom before?" Yeah. In fact, go do it again, please.

I nod. "Yeah."

"Well, I go in and there are all these sophomore girls in the bathroom. Two outside and two in the handicapped stall."

Oh, Christine, two to a stall! You've uncovered the school's underground lesbian ring! I've got to leave! Jeremy needs to know!

I really don't need to hear about this.

"That's weird." I say this with a mildly concerned expression to match hers.

"Yeah, and, like, the other stall was broken, so I had to wait for them and they were taking *forever*."

I nod slowly. Okay. You may continue.

"And two of their friends were *outside* with me. And they were fixing their hair in the mirror."

Unnecessary details. You're wasting air. Get to the gratuitous sex part. I try not to sigh in boredom.

"And they were taking *so* long!" You already said that. "So finally, I was like, 'Hey, I have to use the bathroom!' because, you know, I had to." Duh. "And their friends were like, 'Come on guys, you're taking too long. Let's go!'" Observant little lesbians, aren't they? "So they finally came out." Smoking cigarettes? She puts her hand on mine and suddenly looks as if she is about to inform me of the apocalypse. "They were in there *throwing up*." Oh God, no! Not bulimia! I nod casually.

I say: "It happens." Because it does.

"But, Lis, that's *disgusting*!"

"How else do you think they stay so thin?"

Thin. Maybe you should try it.

"Well, I don't know. But why did they need two to a stall?"

Didn't you ever see *Heathers*?

"To hold each other's hair back?" I mean to say this as a guess, but the question mark gets lost in my attempt to seem unfazed. She takes it as if I'm stating a fact.

"I can't believe that!" You just witnessed it. Believe it. I shrug.

"Welcome to High School."

Some people shouldn't be allowed out of the house.

KATIE

History.

Someone is whispering.

"Lissa! "

I turn around to look.

Lauren.

What?

She mouths something and points to Katie.

I can't understand her. I furrow my eyebrows.

What?

She smiles and mouths more slowly, pointing to Katie again.

She's pissing me off. She's so snobby!

I nod and smile. I get it.

I point to myself.

I agree.

Then, I point to Jeremy.

So does he.

We smile at each other. Katie looks up from between

us. She smiles uncomfortably.

"What?" She looks at both of us. We smile and I turn back up front. I hear her behind me. "What's going on?"

Jeremy looks at me, Katie, and then Lauren, and shakes his head.

Shut up.

I look down at my notebook and realize I've completely lost the lecture. I decide to inform Jeremy of the recent events. I rip a piece of paper from my notebook and write: *"She's pissing me off. She's so snobby!"—Lauren*

I sign it *M.* I fold it and toss it on Jeremy's desk. I look forward again, trying to pick up on what is being said. I hear a laugh next to me. Fuck it. I look at Jeremy and smile. He points to the note with a grin.

She said this?

I nod.

He holds his hands out briefly.

When?

I point backwards at her.

Just now.

Lauren has been watching. He turns and points to the note, nods, then gives Lauren a thumbs-up. She smiles. He leans back so he's not talking directly through Katie. He whispers.

"I think so too."

I suddenly see what is unfolding. I look at Lauren. I look at Jeremy. I grin. "This is too good." They look at me. I pull my pen cap off and write *KATIE* in my notebook. Jeremy raises his eyebrows and smiles. "Lauren.

Bitch and destroyer of writer's block." Lauren gives me
a thumbs-up.

Katie looks up again. Conspiracy in History class. She
holds up her hands.

WHAT IS GOING ON?

We turn forward.

Hah.

MOM

"I think we need to talk."

Again.

I'm already out of the room when she says that. The
dishwasher is going in the kitchen. Maybe I didn't hear
her. I close my bedroom door. She opens it.

"The best way to get a retreat from my children." She
laughs.

Ha, fucking ha, bitch.

"What?" I was innocently walking away when your
voice was drowned out by the dishwasher, I swear.

"I said, we need to talk."

Fuck. Report Card. "Oh?"

"Yeah. Why don't you come into my bedroom?"

Double fuck. I've avoided her successfully for forty-
eight hours and now I'm trapped.

"Okay." I try to reply as innocently as possible. Ds?
What Ds?

I follow her into the bedroom and sit down on the

Laz-E-Boy just because she offers me a spot on the bed next to her. I fold my legs under me and start braiding my hair.

"Will you look at me?"

"What?" I look at her through several sections of hair.

"Stop doing that."

"Kay." I leave the hair in front of my face.

"Be rational."

I shrug. *What?*

"What?"

She shakes her head.

"What's been going on with you and Katie?"

I'm suddenly very relieved and I move the hair out of my face. Stuff. Lots of stuff.

"She's been kinda nasty to everyone lately."

"Oh?"

"Yeah."

"Does this have anything to do with how much time you've been spending with Jeremy lately?"

What time? It hasn't been *that* much time. Has it?

"No."

"They *did* used to go out, didn't they?"

"Yeah."

"And when did they break up?"

"I dunno...October?"

"Oh. Because you know, she has been a very good friend to you for so long, I'd hate to see you lose her."

Yeah, me too. But the person I'm friends with seems to be missing.

"She's been really different lately. She's been nasty to everyone and just sort of ignoring me."

"Are you sure it isn't you?"

"Believe me, mom."

"Maybe you should talk to her."

I don't know how.

"A few people have already tried."

"And?"

And nothing.

"And she was better for a few days. Then she was nasty again."

"Oh. Are you sure this has nothing to do with Jeremy?"

"She was my best friend, she was Jeremy's best friend. Suddenly, she wasn't anymore and we had no one. It was sort of a result of her actions."

She nods.

"I was kinda dependent on her for everything." I really was. "And I recognize that wasn't healthy, but there was nothing I knew to do about it." Helpless. "I thought it was just me she was ignoring, but Lisa's been friends with her since kindergarten and she's ignoring Lisa too."

I pause to find my direction. "It all started around the time she and Jeremy broke up. She had no reason for breaking up with him—"

I sigh. I don't really want to tell this story. As many times as I've asked Katie for her side, she hasn't said a word about her reasons. "Stupid stuff. She told him that it was because he wasn't acting like a real boyfriend."

Stupid stuff.

My mom nods. I'm boring myself. "The point is—we started hanging out *after* she started ignoring us."

"Shouldn't you talk to her about that yourself? She's been a good friend to you. She deserves the same." I nod thoughtfully.

"When they were going out, she told Jeremy that she didn't want to tell me anything 'cause she thinks I have enough of my own problems." You're one of them. I sit in my own uncomfortable silence for a moment.

"You know, Lis, guys can come and go in life, but friends like Katie are friends you'll have for the rest of your life. You really should try and see what's wrong."

I sigh. She doesn't understand. She's too focused on Jeremy. He has nothing to do with this.

"I know, mom. We're just growing apart, I guess. It happens."

I suddenly want to call her.

My mom looks as if she's taking all I have said into consideration and I'm finally getting relaxed.

"So what do you have to say about your report card?"

Ambushed.

DAD

The joys of report cards. My mom just tried her quarter-annual, report-card talk. I pull into my dad's driveway. I didn't pack anything for the weekend and I leave my books in the car. Last time she tried to give her report-card talk, I ran away for two days. This time, I'm not planning on scaring anyone. I go inside.

"Hello—" I look around for signs of human life.

Dad is on the phone and sees me. "Oh!" he says and then cuts himself short. I put a finger to my mouth and he nods.

Who is it?

He takes the receiver away from his face and mouths *Mom.*

I nod and make a cutting motion with my hand. *I'm not here.* As far as she is concerned, I'm never anywhere. He nods and keeps talking. I can hear her yelling through the phone. His side is only a series of "Okay"s. I'm assuming she's upset. If she's upset, it's because of me.

He hangs up. We don't talk about their conversation.

"How was your week?"

"Mom tried to talk about my report card." He nods.

"How'd you do?" He looks worried. I hate disappointing him.

"Not well."

"Okay." He's not sure what else to say.

"I have a bad habit of cutting second marking period. Happens every year. Doesn't help my grades, really."

He nods. At least I'm being honest.

"Is this going to affect college?"

"They only get my final transcript. I just better work my ass off the next two marking periods."

"Why do you think you do this?"

I have to defend myself *again*. There is no defense, really. I just don't care sometimes.

"I don't know. I care, but sometimes, I stop caring."

He nods. He's not perfect either.

"Mom said I should go get counseling for that. I asked her if she cared all the time when she was in high school. She said she was in the top ten-percent of her class." She really said that.

He smiles. "Yeah, but *was* she?"

Good question. I laugh slightly. "I dunno. Last marking period, she said she barely graduated." She really said that, too.

He shakes his head. "Whatever is convenient for her."

"She tried to give me a pep talk. I don't need a pep talk. I'm just getting tired of high school. She tried to tell me how she worked her ass off to get her degree the last four years and how she's at the top of her class and all that. I don't *need* that. If I were forty-six, I'd be at the top, too. And I'm *not* forty-six."

"No, you're not."

Good thing, too.

"She's had forty-six years to learn things. Let me make mistakes."

"Well, hopefully not *too* many mistakes."

"Right." He *is* right, after all. "It's not like I don't care. I get really upset when I don't do well." I really do. "But I slack off anyway." I do that, too. "So I'm not sure *what* that means." Who would be?

My dad shrugs. He doesn't know. And that's the end. We won't talk about this again until I need to. Probably next marking period.

He acknowledges the end by smiling. "It's nice to see you, sweetheart."

I love him.

Especially since he loves me.

I smile too.

CHARLES

American Beauty, fourth time around. It's eleven o'clock at night and I'm ready to get home.

Charles looks at me. I don't look back. I'm flooring it up the on-ramp.

"Don't you think you're going a little fast?"

"No." 55...60...

"Oh. "

Merging...

"I don't think Jeremy likes talking to me anymore."

I nod. "What makes you think that?"

"Now he only calls me for school work."

Hmm. Big hint.

"I think he's tired of talking about computer games."

"But I *like* games!"

"Do you ever talk to anyone about anything other than computers?"

"No."

"What about me?"

"Well, you're different. We talk about life."

"And you can't do that with other people?"

"The guy who writes *Dilbert*, Scott Adams." He pauses and I want to bash my head on the steering wheel. Fucking Dilbert. He continues after a moment of silence. "He says that engineers say what is needed and nothing more. We don't like chit-chat." You're not an engineer, you're a senior in high school. Get over it.

"So you get pissed off when you talk to me?" Mock-insult.

"No. Like I said, you're different."

"You gotta learn to talk to other people like you talk to me."

"Maybe I don't want to."

"Okay, fine."

I laugh. He makes me laugh. "All right." Ice is broken.

"You know," He pauses, "I thought Jeremy was going to ask you out."

I smile at this. "Really? Why would you think something like that?"

"I dunno. He's always looking for you. It's just something I noticed." He's a quick one.

"Oh. Yeah, I guess we're spending some time together. We're not gonna go out, though. Geeze! What made you bring *that* up?" I can't help but laugh.

"I don't know anything about relationships. I was just kinda curious how you would respond."

I laugh even harder. "What a question! Don't worry. I don't know anything about them either. Never had one in my life."

He smiles. "Well, that's different."

"What? For me? Nah. No one's ever asked me out. Simple as that."

"Me neither."

"I know—you gotta learn to talk about more than just computers."

"Ev likes computers." Ev is his love. She lives in Taiwan.

"Yeah, but what's that to base a relationship on? Huh?" I'm still laughing periodically .

"I dunno. I'd do anything for her."

"Yeah, but that's a sad existence. We need to find you someone."

"We?"

"Yeah, we. We'll get you a nice girl to settle down with." I'm still giggling. I'm finding myself deliriously funny.

"Ev is nice." His suggestion. I laugh even harder. Not at him. I'm just laughing at this point.

"Pomona is nice this time of year." That's where Ev is applying to college. Damn, I'm funny.

"I know, I know."

"Go after her!"

"I would but—"

"Come on! Throw caution to the wind! Pomona has very *nice* wind."

He sighs, laughing, but frustrated. I turn on my blinker to get off the highway. Time to go home. It gets quiet.

"You could go out with someone if you wanted." He's talking about Jeremy. He's talking about Eric. He might even be talking about himself. I play dumb.

"Who? John? Yeah, but I'd never ask him out." John's cute. I don't know much else about him. He's my token crush.

He shakes his head. "I'll do it for you!"

"Will you? Really?" Three-quarters of me would love this. I could eliminate all this Jeremy stuff in one fell swoop. And I'd be a heck of a lot less confused.

"Yeah. I see him sometimes."

"Do it." I'm serious for the moment.

"Okay."

"Good."

I start laughing again. "Or just tell him I'd fuck him."

He buries his head in his hands. I'm too much.

"So is that what you think about in school all day?"

I stop laughing. "No. There's a lot of stuff I *do* think about—sex isn't really one of them." I pause, wanting to tread lightly. "Why, what do you think about?"

"Well..." He stops.

"Ev?"

"Yeah, of course."

Of course.

"All the time?"

"Yeah." He smiles. I can feel it. I don't even have to look at him. "But I didn't tell you *what* I think about."

Oh god. I almost swerve into a mailbox. I know what he's going to say. I just pray he doesn't say it.

"What?"

"Her tying me to my bed."

Goodbye, mailbox. I slam on the brakes. He's laughing.

"I didn't need to hear that."

He's still laughing. We're stopped in the middle of the street.

"Did I surprise you?"

No, actually. "No. I kind of expected it." You horny little geek-boy. Jesus!

"Then why'd you stop like that?

"I didn't want to hit a mailbox." I say this with what I'm sure is some sort of bizarre grin.

He's laughing harder. I ease on the gas again. We're both laughing, and I'm shaking my head. Good lord, what a weird conversation.

After that, there's little to say and despite my occasional "Oh God..." upon the realization of what has been said, and some momentary laughter, there is silence.

I pull into his driveway and he looks at me.

I sigh. There's a million things I want to say to an unbiased ear.

"I don't like Jeremy." Now there's a weird one..

Charles gives a short laugh. "What? So you love him?"

I shake my head. "No. I like him as a friend. I don't *like* him, though."

He nods. "Do you think he feels the same?"

"Yeah. I'm pretty sure of it."

So why do we keep hooking up? I don't say that.

"Okay—I don't know what to say to that."

"You're not supposed to. I didn't finish my thought." So why do we keep hooking up?

"Okay. What was the rest of your thought?" So why do we keep hooking up?

"I dunno if I want to finish it." So why do we keep hooking up?

"If you want to finish it, go ahead." So why do we keep hooking up?

"No. I don't think I do." Silence. He looks like he expects something. If it were Jeremy, this would be the point that we'd—

"Goodnight." I hear myself say this abruptly. Get out. Before I mistake you for someone else.

He nods and looks as if he feels his evening isn't complete. "This is when I get out, huh?"

"Uh...yeah. We're at your house." I suddenly feel badly that I'm being so abrupt. "Do you want me to call?"

"Tonight?"

"Yeah, sure. I have to wait up for Em to call anyway. She's at a party and I have to pick her up at around one. Might as well spend my time constructively."

He shakes his head. "No. Maybe later this week."

I nod. "Sure." Now it's me that feels rejected. "Sure."

"I'll talk to you later." He doesn't get out of the car. He just looks at me. So why do we keep hooking up?

"Goodnight."

He gets out of the car and slams the door.

So why do we keep—
He walks up to his front door and I pull away.
You whore.

FEEDBACK

"But I *want* to put you in."
He shakes his head
"Oh, come on. I'll just use your name. I have a feed-back section and the person is nameless. You don't even have to say anything important. It's already been said for you."
"No, it's okay."
"No, really, it's not a problem."
"Don't worry about it."
I nod. All right, all right.
"Eric's coming home this weekend." I volunteer this because it makes me happy.
He shakes his head again. "Then I suppose you'll be busy on Friday."
"Not till later. I got a new rug for my room. I wouldn't protest too violently if I had company picking it up."
He shrugs. "It's something to do."
"Yeah. But I want to be back by seven. ETA is eight o'clock sharp."
"Ah. Okay. Right. *Er-ic.*" He smiles.
"Shut up!" I hit him lightly. "You just wish you were as perfect."

"Uh-huh."

I shake my head. "Shut up."

"I didn't say anything!"

"I know. You were going to though."

He smiles "And how do you know what that was?"

"I just know. I have a keen sense of...knowing... stuff..."

"Uh-huh, right. You wish."

"Shut up!"

"Okay, okay! I understand. I won't say anything more."

"Shut up, you know I'm kidding."

"You better be careful, or else people are gonna stop talking to you and you're gonna wonder why."

The only reply I seem to have for this is: "Shut up!"

I'm frustrated and we laugh.

And then we don't say anything. We're walking. On grass. Across the municipal soccer field. Towards town. I'm happy.

Eric. "Have you ever been in love?" I love Eric.

"Shut up!"

I'm never living that down. "No, I'm serious."

"Okay. I don't know then. I think I was."

"'Cause I was just wondering."

"Why?"

"I thought maybe you might know how to tell."

"What?"

"If something is love."

"I might. How long?"

"Six years?"

He nods. "You're in love." He says this with authority.

"You sure? How do you know?"

"Are you stupid?"

"Well, I thought maybe it was just a really long crush."

"No. Crushes don't last that long."

"Oh. Okay."

"Does he know?"

"No."

"Are you stupid?"

Shut up!

MOM

ERIC.

I'm picking at a slice of pizza.

I'm also sitting at a kitchen table.

Then my mom walks in. I close the file I'm working in and look at her.

"What?"

She stands in the doorway and looks at me.

"What?" I repeat this.

"Oh, I don't know. I'm just looking at you. You're so pretty sometimes."

Sometimes.

"Uh...yeah. I'm gonna go back to work."

"You don't realize how pretty you are, do you?"

"No, guess not." I'm short in my answers. I'm slightly

annoyed. I hate interruptions when I'm composing.

"What are you working on?"

"Essay. For English. We have to write a science fiction story." What I should really be working on. I add: "Pain in the ass. Don't want to ruin my concentration."

"Okay. I'll just watch you work"

Nooo... It doesn't work that way.

"Mom..."

She looks at me. "Have you seen your face lately?"

"Mommm...."

"No, really. It looks terrible...You know, you can take medication for bad acne like you have."

"Mom, I don't have bad acne. It's just a breakout."

"I know, but you get pimples a lot."

"Mom, I'm a teenager."

"And you don't want to take birth control pills for it or anything."

"MOM." I almost shout this.

I do have to admit, my skin has been bad.

"Have you still been taking those laxatives?"

"Only sometimes."

Three times a day.

"You know, those things dehydrate you. It can really ruin your skin."

"I don't think that's the problem. It's just a breakout."

I sigh. I don't want to deal with this. I need them. To lose weight.

She sighs too. "All right..."

I raise my eyebrows and go back to pretending to

write a science fiction story. She continues to stand there.

"May I help you?"

"Were there any calls for me while I was out?"

"Jon called for Emily three times, but other than that, no calls."

Jon is Chris' replacement. He calls five times a day. Really. Emily is glad to be going out with him because he had no friends and now he has one. Really.

She sighs and looks up at the ceiling.

"You know, I don't want to date Ethan."

What happened to Mike?

I don't ask this. "Um...who's Ethan, mom?"

"You know, Ethan. From the bike club."

"Oh." I still don't know who Ethan is. "Then don't go out with him."

"Yeah, I guess. It's just—I don't want to date *anyone* right now."

"Then don't." Duh.

"But if I don't date *someone*, I may never go out with anyone again."

Huh?

"Okay then, fine. Date him."

"I don't know."

"Mom, if you don't want to do something, then don't do it. It doesn't make sense. No one is holding a gun to your head and telling you to date people."

She looks at me and back up at the ceiling and I can tell she didn't listen to a word I just said. I don't think the idea ever occurred to her, and now that I've mentioned it, she's probably written it off as immature.

"I don't know..." She wanders back out into the hall. She looks lost.

I go back to my story. The phone rings. Sick of interruptions, I ignore it. Emily is at track practice and my mom is still lost. The answering machine decides to intervene.

"Emily, It's Jon..."

The closest large object to me is Nellie Bly's biography. I throw it at the door in the hopes that it will shut. When it does nothing but fall sadly short of the door, I get up and close it myself and move my night table in front of it.

Where are...earplugs...earplugs.

"So how's life?"

Eric.

ERIC

I'm picking at a slice of pizza.

I'm also sitting at a kitchen table.

Did I mention I was nervous?

"So how's life?"

Eric.

"Life's fine. Life's life. Did you get the birthday present I sent you?" I remind myself I'm on a mission.

"Yeah. I've got so much *reading* to do, though. It's like, they fill your head with all these *words* you're never going to use again. I'm completely exhausted. I'll read the books you gave me when finals are over. I've been meaning to read *American Psycho*."

I smile. I gave him two books. *American Psycho* and *All The Pretty Horses*. The latter is my favorite. The former was filler.

"It's an...interesting book." I pause. Do it. Now. "I was wondering...if I could ask you a question."

"Ask." He re-adjusts his chair.

"Well, I know it's kind of far in advance, but I figured if you weren't doing anything of consequence on the weekend of June second, you'd maybe hypothetically consider coming to a prom?"

"A senior prom?"

"A junior seems a bit young for you."

"Your senior prom?"

"Well, that would certainly work out. Mine just happens to fall on the second."

"With you?"

"If you had someone else in mind, I could deal with it..." I watch his expression. "...but I wouldn't protest if you'd consider going with me." Exhale, darling.

He's smiling. "Of course."

Six years and it was that easy?

"Can I ask *you* a question now?"

I nod, lifting the pizza to my mouth. A catch?

"Can't you go with someone in your class?"

I nod again, chewing. No catch. Of course I can, but why? I've got you!

"Have you asked anyone from your class?"

I shake my head, still chewing.

"So..." He's waiting for an explanation with an interested smile.

I swallow. "I asked you first—before anyone else."

He nods. "Why?"

"Because they're not you. I dunno. I have my reasons."

"And these reasons are..."

I smile. He's so dense, I just want to hug him. "Nothing of consequence."

"All right." He shakes his head and laughs.

ANNA

I'm sitting on the side of a small hill, tossing handfuls of pebbles down the slope into the scattered piles of leaves and snow below me. A foot or two away, Jeremy is doing the same. It's Friday, so I guess wasting sunlight is a luxury we can spare on a late February afternoon.

"It's funny—a month ago, I think, I went out with Charles. We saw a movie. Anyway, we were talking and he said something—he said he thought you were going to ask me out."

"Really?"

"Yeah. He said it was 'cause you were—and I swear to God, this is exactly what he said—it seemed like you were always looking for me."

"I guess I am sometimes."

"Yeah."

"What'd you say to that?"

"I just laughed—told him I thought that was funny. Of course not!"

"You still feel that way?"

I didn't feel that way even when I'd said it at first. I wanted it.

"Mmm-hmm." I look at him.

"What?"

"Nothing."

"No, what? You're thinking something."

He always does this. How does he know?

"No, it's nothing, I swear." I laugh uncomfortably.

"It's not nothing, Lis. Tell me what you're thinking."

"Jeremy, it's nothing."

He moves closer and tries to look at me. I'm avoiding looking at him.

"It's never nothing. You always think about everything. Come on."

"No. It's okay."

"Just start with something. I'll wait."

I take a soft breath. "You know that Counting Crows song? I think it's track five."

"On their first album?"

"Yeah. I think it's called 'Anna Begins.'"

I've been listening to it on repeat lately.

He nods. "I think I know it. How does it go?"

I try to speak melodically—singing is not something I

want to do. "Kindness falls like rain...it washes me away...
Oh lord, I'm not ready for this sort of thing. Something
like that."

"I guess."

"Oh, well, I was just thinking. It reminds me of you."

He laughs. "Oh wait. I think I know. Isn't that the one
where he don't get no sleep?"

I smile too. "Yeah, but that's not why it reminds me
of you."

"Oh. All right then." He doesn't get it.

"Never mind. It was just a silly thought."

"That was it?"

"Mostly, yeah."

"You sure?"

"Well, that and... You remember freshman year?
When Katie tried to set you up with that girl who skis?"

"Yeah. I didn't really like her."

"Well, I had this crush on you that same time...I was
kinda jealous."

"You're serious?"

"Yeah. I just didn't say anything. I thought Katie—I
don't know what I thought. I just figured maybe it'd go
away, so I didn't say anything."

"Did it?"

"Yeah. I just didn't think about it."

"Huh."

"Of course that has nothing to do with now—I just
kind of wanted to tell you. Different me, different you."

"Okay." he nods. "Thanks."

"You're welcome." It's the only reply I can think of.

"You shouldn't let Katie tell you what to think."

"She didn't. She wasn't—I was just...embarrassed. I told her later—sophomore year."

"What'd she say?"

"Nothing."

"How about when we were going out?"

"Oh, that was fine. I told you, I was over it."

I thought they were cute. A little weird, but cute.

"Oh. You're silly sometimes, you know that? You think about things too much."

"I don't—I think just enough for what is required. I think about what I'm going to say before I say it. I plan. Doesn't everyone?"

"I don't. I just say what I think."

"You're different."

He laughs and shakes his head.

"I asked Eric to the prom this weekend."

Brief silence. "Lissa's trophy date." And then, "I don't know who I'm going with yet. "

The thought doesn't occur to me until later that maybe he had it in the back of his mind that we might go.

This is what occurs to me now: "Please don't go with Katie." I guess this is jealousy.

"Of course not."

"Oh, I didn't know. I thought you mentioned it before."

He presses his lips together and looks at me.

"You cold?"

The sun is below the trees.

"Not really." I lie.

"You're shaking. You want to go back?"

"Do you?"

"I could stay out, but you're cold, so we're going back."

"No, it's okay. We can stay if you want."

"That's silly. Come on."

We get up and I dust off my pants.

On the way back, I scratch my right arm on a birch tree during a game of tag. He caught me against the tree and I was so afraid he was going to kiss me, I swung around it, dragging my arm across a twig.

Funny thing is, all I wanted right then was a kiss.

When he pointed my injury out in the car later, I told him I didn't remember where it came from.

"That's so weird. I don't even remember it."

"Does it hurt?" It did. For three days.

"No. Didn't even notice it till you said something."

Monday morning, Katie noticed it too.

My reply: "Huh... I didn't even notice it until you said something."

KEVIN

I never feel well fourth period.

"I think she should be a bisexual."

"You think it should get *more* complicated?"

"It would make it more interesting. Or at least make

her a closet lesbian."

"Okay, okay, but I'm trying to keep it real."

"Have you watched Jerry Springer lately?"

"I said *real*."

"All right, all right. Calm down."

"What if she were your friend?"

Kevin looks at the packet of paper and flips through.

"I'm not sure I'd want a friend like this. Too high maintenance."

I try to laugh, but my stomach feels like...I have no analogy. It just feels yucky.

"No, really."

"Really?" He becomes serious. "Well, do you see what she's doing to herself?"

"Yeah." I pause and exhale. I do *not* feel well. "It goes on in this school all the time—If you knew her, what would you say?"

He pauses and looks at me. I must look absolutely pale. I watch him blink twice. My heart moves slowly to either my stomach or my throat. Maybe my stomach rejected it and tossed it into my throat. I can't tell.

"She—Melissa—I'd tell her..." He looks at me again and then takes a soft breath. His expression has changed. "Be careful. It's not healthy."

I nod. "I know."

He hands the story back to me. "You don't need this."

"You said it was good."

"I love it. I think it's great."

"But if people love it..."

"Do you love it?"

"Yes. She's the best character I've written. I need to finish this."

"It's not all true."

I nod. "It makes good fiction."

"Then make it just that."

"I can't. I have to write it this way."

"Then don't write it anymore."

"But it's the best..."

"Sacrifice?"

"*Experiment* in writing. And yes, sacrifice a little if I have to. Writing is what I want to do. I want to try this. I've got to finish it."

"I care, you know."

"I know."

"A lot of people do."

"I know." I hand the story back to him. "This is your copy."

"What's his name?"

"Does it matter?"

"Do I know him?"

"His name is Jeremy."

He tilts his head and waves the story slightly. "Yeah—so is his."

I feel sick. I want to throw up.

On the floor maybe?

I look at Kevin.

"Am I ugly?"

"You look a little peaked. But no, you're cute."

"No. I mean, am I an ugly person?"

"You can't be."

"Why not?"

"I can't think of how you could be."

"This doesn't make you think any less of me?"

I realize only after I've said it that *this* might need some clarification: the story, the pills, the thing, my need to write the whole mess down.

He shakes his head.

"You just look tired."

"I think I'm gonna puke." I only halfway mean this—right now.

"Oh. Do you want to go to the bathroom?"

"No. I want to hear what you have to say."

He looks at me, so I straighten myself a little. Despite some dizziness.

"Okay—then I'll tell you what I think." He's quite good at being frank. I lean over hoping my stomach will disappear. "I'm jealous. I wish I could write something like this...."

I only half hear this. I have to leave.

On my way into one of the stalls, I pause to look in the mirror. I see a pale girl with bad breakouts and size fourteen jeans—now four months old.

Next time I see her, she has flushed fifty-eight pink pills down the toilet.

If I'm gonna be fat, I might as well have good skin.

MELISSA

I don't really want to talk about it.

"Do you want a blow job?"

There's no respectable way for me to have asked it. But then again, it's not a respectable act.

"That's kind of hard for me to answer right now."

I had to take my hand out of his pants when his mom called a few minutes later. We talked briefly before he left. I just wanted to hug him. I felt silly. I felt like a little girl. I didn't want him to go. I felt so exposed. I wanted someone to hold me. I wanted someone to take care of me.

He left the next day.

Vacation.

That's how my February break began.

I haven't really talked to him much since.

I had asked Lauren's advice:

"How far is too far?"

She told me that it's always too far unless I think I love someone. I told myself I didn't love him and wouldn't— at least not in that sense. I respect him. I knew that. I also knew we shouldn't do this unless we were more than friends. In most senses, we weren't.

So I reverted to someone else: Melissa before the library. Katie and I suddenly became pals again. Jeremy was just Jeremy again. There was no climax, no big moral. No winners, no losers, no villains, no heroes. There was just me and an unfinished story.

I tried to finish it officially. I tried starting some sort

of conversation, but figuring out the difference between avoidance and indifference with Jeremy was beyond me, so I buried it in my mind. I'm not sure what I would have said to him anyway. I wanted to cry—I had wanted something more and that's why I didn't want it to happen again. I didn't want to not feel anything but empty. He made me happy. I guess the thought of him still does.

No one ever asked me if I liked who I had become or what I had created.

Everyone thought of this as my fictional creation—even if they knew.

To be perfectly honest, I like the person I became after this—or because of it.

She is comfortable in her own skin.

She is also in love with this story.

Strange.

I guess she was bound to find love somewhere.

Jeremy might've been right when he said that I think too much about everything.

"From, like, November until, oh, March, if you wanted to find Jeremy, you just had to find Melissa." Katie says this with no emotion. It's a fact, I guess.

I smile. "Yeah. And then I ran out of things to say to him. There was nothing more to say." I don't mention that I just couldn't find the words for any of it. Embarrassed, inevitable, finished, love, respect, think, value, we, us, me, you —friendship.

She shrugs. "When me and Jeremy broke up, I would walk through the halls and see him and I wouldn't know what to do. But now, he's just Jeremy again—the one who threw green Jell-O at me freshman year. It's okay now." She smiles and kicks at the wood chips we happen to be standing in.

I'm digging a shallow hole in the dirt with my heel. "That's good."

Thank you.

EPILOGUE(S)

KATIE

Lissy—

I'm sure I'm supposed to respond to your story. Beyond the fact that I thought it was a literary masterpiece, I'm stuck for words. It reminded me of something wonderfully stream-of-conscience (however you spell that) like Vonnegut or Faulkner—but more Lissy.

So, with literary accolades put aside, the story made me want to vomit. That old feeling, the deep pit in my stomach that aches with some great hurt. Maybe regret. Maybe shame. Maybe embarrassment. Probably all of those things.

I know that you deserved better than the treatment you got. And that I am (or was) Katie, the sometimes bitch that did a little more than shut out as many people as I could to just try and survive 2nd and 3rd marking period. So did I ever stop caring about you? No. Did I stop trying as hard as I should have? Yes. Guess that's why I'm in therapy.

I guess I'm wallowing in my own self-pity. Sorry—but I can't help it. Just another response to your story. I should have broken up with Jeremy better. I shouldn't have had an internal breakdown where I decided that I couldn't be anyone's security blanket anymore.

You know Lassie and White Fang? The guy really cares about the dog but yells at it to make it run away and live on it's own. Bad analogy. I know—but you should be used to it by now.

Maybe how I feel is a little better and the need to vomit has passed. Could've been this little fan letter that I wrote you. Maybe it was the American Girls Catalogue that my English teacher just passed around the class.

Lissy, I'm sorry. I should have been different. I shouldn't have been named after a bitch, I should have been named after a best friend that cared a great deal and never stopped loving her friend. And no matter what happens, I'm not going to stop thinking you're great. When I said I was embarrassed, it was for my behavior, not yours. Strange that we have Jeremy in common. Not good or bad. Just bizarre. (Your word again!)

So that's it—my letter of shoulds. Regrets. Pride—that someone I know is so gifted. I'm a mess.

The End

Love,

Katie

ERIC

It's been almost two years. A week away from almost two years. I feel like I should have a party—it's the end, I can start to edit.

Really, I'm just sitting on my bunk bed in my dorm room. No parties. It's 9:37 in the morning. I have nowhere to be except here and no one here would know how to celebrate this, anyway. Lauren is in California, Jeremy is in Vermont, Charles is in Missouri, Katie is in New Jersey. I am here.

We were in the garage, I believe. A few hundred feet away from the end of the driveway. You all remember the driveway, right?

It took me almost a week to say the words "So, what did you think of my story?"

I wanted to choke and cry and dance and run. He only looked at me and I only stood there. He looked longer than necessary and I stood silently because that was the only thing I could do. He inhaled, he exhaled. A halfhearted "It was good" floated towards me. I nodded and said something thoughtful as if I understood that what he had said was the most meaningful piece of literary criticism I'd heard. He liked the dialogue—everyone likes the dialogue. He didn't really remember the characters' names—no one remembers the character's names. He didn't really like it, actually—he's the first one to be honest. I want to tell him this but it would sound like I was fishing for a compliment. I want to kiss the top of his

head and jump and clap. He didn't like it. I feel the need
to thank him excessively for not liking it—thank him for
even bothering to form an opinion. I ask what I can fix.

"Those sections, where people say what they think
about the story? Pointless. You should take them out." I
did that this morning. I took out two.

"Especially that one with Melissa and that guy where
they're talking about the rug. Take that one out." I leave
that one in. It's about him. He doesn't know that I need
it. He doesn't know it's not finished. He knows it's about
him though. He doesn't let me know he knows. But we
both know.

"The main problem I saw—and I have this problem
in my writing too—my professors points this out all the
time—is that there's no *real conflict*." I understand. We
leave it at that. We drop it. We're still in the garage.

What you didn't see:

I love you.

I love you, too. But not like that.

This doesn't hurt because all I wanted was to say it
once. Because it took all these pages to say it. Because I
couldn't say it any other way.

A Million Miles Up

WHILE WE WERE HUNTING RABBITS

"Tell me a story."

"Not tonight, Elly. It's getting late. I have a calc test in the morning."

"You never study anyway!

"Only since you've been around."

"So I *have* been a good influence."

I look at her. And then crack a smile. "You're a crazy mofo."

"So tell me a story!"

"Okay, okay. Then you have to get out and go into your house so I can go home and look at my calc notes and assess exactly how screwed I am."

"Aw, you're the best."

"I know, I know. Okay, a story. So, once upon a time, there was an enchantingly beautiful, witty princess named Eleanor who wanted with all her heart to be a... sculptor. She took secret lessons from the best sculptor in her kingdom—but in secret because her father didn't think women should be doing anything besides sitting and looking pretty. And while Eleanor was *ravishingly* beautiful, she would rather create beautiful things than just sit and rely on her own prettiness... which she knew might someday fade."

"Hey, you're good at this."

"Are you going to listen or not? No interruptions."

"Geez, sorry, Aesop."

"One day, Eleanor went out disguised as a courtier with her father's hunting party. While all the men were chasing foxes and whatever all over God's creation, Eleanor got distracted by a peculiar little rabbit that was hopping around in the forest. She decided she wanted it for a pet—or at least a companion, so she went off to fetch it."

"If she follows it into a hole and meets a smiling cat and a smoking caterpillar, I'm going to be very disappointed."

"Shhh. Artist at work, here."

"Sorry."

"So she goes after it—she loved rabbits. And she follows it and gets completely fucking lost. Like, there is no finding her way home and it's already dark and she's thinking she's pretty screwed, right? When, suddenly, she stumbles on a large clearing and she sees, under the moonlight, hundreds—thousands—millions—of fluffy, white rabbits feeding under the sky. The stars were shining like diamonds and she saw a man walking through the field towards her. She was so afraid it was a thief or something, she didn't move an inch and just let him approach her. He came all the way up to her and removed his hood and it was the sculptor. He said, *Until I met you, I was like a boat lost on the ocean. You're the reason I am and the reason for me to continue to be.* And some other sickeningly sweet stuff that made the princess melt into a little gob of prettiness."

"Awwwwww!"

I can't help but smile. She's curled up on the front seat watching me. A little gob of prettiness in the moonlight.

"And he carried her off and they took one of the king's boats and sailed it to the ends of the earth where they found Easter Island and spent the rest of their days carving huge rectangular faces on the rocks on the island and being in love and stuff. The end."

"That was a nice story, Scott."

"Thank you."

"It's too bad you don't have any rabbits following you around."

I look at her. "Sometimes, if my shoes are untied, my laces follow me around."

"You know, in a weird way, I wish that were good enough."

Pause. "Me too."

In a minute, I will watch her walk across her lawn.

And fight the urge to rob a pet store.

LOVE

Ain't love the sweetest thing.

Gayest thing. It's gay. My mom was not pleased with me using that term the other night. I told her that the meatloaf she made with ground turkey was gay. She made a face. I made a face. It went something like this:

"Scott, I made this meatloaf with ground turkey since dad's on a diet."

"Mom, that's gay."

What are they teaching you at that school?

Money rule the world. Bitches make the world go round.

I realized only after the fact that it was silly to be rebellious about meatloaf. Like love, I was being gay.

What does U2 know about love anyway?

Elly took a long draw off a twice-lit Parliament and had this to say:

"Bono knows about love because belly dancers are about love. He loves belly dancers. I read that in *Rolling Stone* once."

I asked her: "How are belly dancers about love?"

"Because love is bullshit. It's all about getting it up and jerking it off. Having an exposed navel helps with that sort of stuff."

I reached for her hand with an open palm. "Gimme."

She handed me the cigarette and I held it close to my cheek for a minute before speaking.

"I think love is gay." This was my first attempt at this thesis.

"Don't just hold it. Smoke it!"

I put it to my mouth and did a quick in and out.

"Okay. You mean, like, love is metaphorical sodomy?"

"Wha...no! It's just dumb. You give girls pink stuff on Valentine Day and I can never remember anyone's birthday and I wouldn't be caught dead buying a teddy bear."

I paused to take a drag. "And it makes you do dumb things like chase people. Just 'cause you want to be near them. Dumb."

"Ah." She exhaled. "Okay. I think I get it." She reached for the cigarette and I handed it back to her. "I liked metaphorical sodomy better."

We both fell silent and looked at the jungle gym a few wood-chipped feet away from the swings we were sitting on. She turned to hand me the cigarette after a minute of silence. I turned at the same time and kissed her.

She punched me in the mouth.

Then, she threw her head back and laughed.

As much as my face hurt, I stayed where I was and watched her close her eyes and stretch her mouth back into a broken grin.

She said, her shoulders bouncing lightly up and down, "Ah, like father, like daughter."

The next day, she killed her dad.

ELLY

So, I went to a party when I was seventeen. I did that a lot. We had something we liked to call Wiper Fluid. It was all parts whatever each of us could sneak into my friend, Jerry's, basement. Add a little blue dye to make it festive (although it often just made it ugly). Mix together in oversize Tupperware containers. Drink large quantities until standing is a surreal experience.

I spent most of that night going between the snack table and trying to feel up Jerry's girlfriend, who could get wasted on just about anything. Even mouthwash. I swear to God.

"Scott, you know, I think I'm *drunk.*" She told me this after sweeping her arms around my neck and trying to hang off it in a quasi-slow-dance sort of fashion. I raised my arms, trying to hold her up while slipping my hand up her sweater, searching for something to grab.

"You're fine. Look! You're still standing!"

Searching, searching...

One side of her mouth went up in a sideways grin and she threw herself backwards onto the couch, taking me with her.

"Not anymore!" She found herself hysterical and pushed me away so she could curl up and giggle. Not having felt anything but a soft cotton-poly blend, I wandered back across the room to eat more cheese puffs and dip. Halfway there, I decided to make a detour to the bathroom. It was then that Elly met me. Or, perhaps, I met Elly. Either way, she made a point of coming between me and the open bathroom door.

"What?" I said this only half seriously. Instead of walking around her, I allowed her to stay in my way.

"What's your problem?" She asked. I thought for a minute. Was she a friend of what's-her- face?

"Uh. Don't have a problem." Except that I had to pee.

"I think you do."

I made an attempt to get around her because I really did have to pee. She kept moving to block me.

"Okay, actually, you're my problem."

She kissed me on the mouth and then nodded.

"You got it, kiddo."

That would be the last time I would touch her until the night we would sit on the swings at the grammar school.

On my way out of the bathroom, I saw her in the corner, one hand holding a red cup and the other down some guy's pants. She paused her activities for a moment to yell across the room to me. She told me to wait outside for her, which I, in the hopes that I would get a repeat performance from her, did.

I had the great pleasure of driving Elly home that night and not laying a finger on her.

"I'm Elly." She said, on her way out of the car.

"Scott," I said, trying to lock eye contact to let her know that I was good to go.

"Pick me up tomorrow, Scott. I want to take a field trip. To the lake."

"Uh."

"At three."

She left my car smelling like Jack Daniels and some other guy's aftershave.

It was that night that Elly began and I ended.

Hello. Nice to meet you.

THE LAKE

"Do you have to smoke those things?" She rolls open the window violently, waving at the air.

"These? I just smoke a few a day." I hold up the pack of Parliaments to demonstrate.

"Gah. Stop. I hate 'em."

"Uh...okay." I chuckle lightly and make no move to put out my cigarette. She leans over me and opens my window as well. A cold rush of winter air hits my face. She settles back into her seat.

"So this is the lake, eh?" She says this, now fidgeting with her jacket zipper.

"Yup."

"I've never been here before."

"So I've heard."

"Mmm."

My sarcasm goes unappreciated. So I offer something less biting: "It's prettier in the summer."

"I can imagine."

"How did you end up there last night?"

"I live down the street. You?"

"I dunno. I just know him."

As I am saying that, she reaches over and takes the cigarette out of my mouth and stamps it out on the half-lowered passenger window. Then, she hands it back to me.

"Don't smoke. It's bad for me."

"Sorry." I take the butt from her, more surprised than

anything else, and flick it out the window. "You go to Centennial?"

"Yes. I'm your year."

"Fuckin A. I've never seen you."

"I'm not there much."

"Ah. That'll do it."

Pause.

She picks up my copy of *Catch-22* from the floor of the passenger's side. "You like Heller?"

"Yeah. I just finished it for the third time."

"I've never read it. I watched the movie."

"Didn't make any sense as a film."

She cracks a smile. "You're one of those people who thinks books should stay books and movies should stay movies."

"No. I just think that in this case—"

"Did Orr make it to Sweden?"

"Of course."

"See, I think he drowned somewhere around the Netherlands."

"Was that even in the movie?"

"Maybe not. But I read the Cliffs Notes, too. For class."

"So you *do* go sometimes." I smile and raise my eyebrows teasingly. Hey, hey, hey. Good looking guy, right here. Come and get him.

She looks down and then out. "Sometimes, yes." She hands the book to me. I look at it and throw it in the back seat, then ease back into my seat and put my arm behind

her headrest. Still thinking of this as a drawn-out version
of the strategy game called "getting head", I play my next
move.

"I've got some gin."

"No." A little bit happy, a little bit naughty.

"Yeah." A little more naughty, a lot bit cocky.

"Do you have anywhere to go tonight?"

"Oh hell no."

"To your house, it is."

To my house it was.

ONE THING YOU NEED TO KNOW

My father, being a great lover of gin, kept a reasonable
stash in the basement liquor closet.

"It's one of those things." I explained to Elly when I
revealed a liquor cabinet full of what might be, on any oc-
casion, Seagram's, Beefeater or Gordon's, but always gin.
"He likes it." And so did we.

"Do you do this a lot?" is what Elly asked when I offered her the bottle.

"Mmm." I nodded, wiping my mouth. She nodded
as well and took a drink. "My dad doesn't notice, I don't
think."

"You like gin?"

"Like father, like son."

She took another, longer drink.

"Like father, like daughter" is what she finally said.

She passed it back to me.

I moved closer to her to retrieve it. She, correspondingly, got up off the couch and wandered into the room.

"You read a lot?" is what she finally said when she made it to the book case at the other end of the room.

"Um. Yeah. Kinda."

"That's cool. Did you read all these?"

"Not all. A lot of. They're my dad's." I got up and walked over to the bookcase and stood behind her as her finger scanned the titles.

"*The Recent Religious History of Kazakhstan? The Handbook of Knots and Splices? The Bell Jar?*"

"Yeah. It's kinda scattered."

She took the bottle from my hand and sat down on the floor by the coffee table books and atlases.

"I used to trace things out of there." I said this when she picked up the world atlas. I surprised myself.

"Trace?"

"You know, like, the different maps. I preferred political to topographic. But if I was feeling artistic..." I faded off and walked away. Weird topic. "Do you like movies?"

"Why'd you trace 'em?"

"I dunno. Something to do. We didn't have cable or a DVD or anything till a year or two ago."

"*What?* How do you live?"

"With air and water and things..."

"*Why* would anyone not have cable?"

"I guess my mom didn't want us watching a lot of TV. I mean, we still had network channels. I like PBS. And we still had *The Simpsons*."

"Do you have brothers? Sisters?" Elly in interrogation mode.

"Sister."

"Does she go to school?"

"Naw. She's married. She's got a cat. Do you like cats?"

"No. I'd kill it if I had one."

"Oh. That's pleasant." I forced a small chuckle.

"Not intentionally. Just, you know, I'd forget to feed it or let it out of the basement or something."

"Oh. My mom takes care of ours."

"You've got one? I wouldn't think you a cat person."

"I'm a skinny white boy who reads too much. I'm definitely not a dog person."

"What's that supposed to mean?"

"I feel like saying I'm a dog person is like saying I just got back from wearing flannel, cleaning my gun and skinning a deer. Or logging the Yukon or something."

"Uh..."

"Yeah, I know, the Yukon isn't big for logging. It's gold. Like I just got back from panning for gold in the Yukon or something."

"Uh, right." She continued to page through the atlas, not paying full attention to me. "I just think they're cute and friendly. I had no idea it implied so much about your manhood." She took an argument-ending swig from the bottle. And then looked back at the atlas.

For lack of anything better to do, I grabbed my crotch and did my best version of a cowboy. "My manhood is

just fine, ma'am." Maybe more of a private-eye voice. I
took my hand off my crotch. "Sorry, uh..."

She put her hand up to her mouth and swallowed.
Then she laughed loudly. "Oh my God, I can't believe
you just did that!" I shrugged. "You don't have to stay
way over there. Here." She held up the bottle and waved
me closer. I walked back and sat down next to her and
the atlases.

I watched her page through Eastern Europe. Then I
noticed her hand.

"Hey. . ." I reached for it and held it in mine for a
second.

"What?"

I pushed the sleeve of her sweatshirt up her forearm.
Big blotches of black and blue.

"Shit, Elly, what'd you do?" I laughed lightly. "Good
job on your arm."

She withdrew it and pushed the sleeve back down.

"Sports."

"What sport do you play?"

"Uh, I don't play on a team or anything."

"Yeah, but, like, what is that? Softball? Basketball? I
never though of you much as someone who plays team
sports. I bet it's boxing." I made some playful jabs at the
air.

"Soccer. I play soccer." She said this coldly.

I stopped jabbing. "With your arms?" This spilled out
of my mouth before my brain could catch it. *Duh*. And I
looked at her. With my mouth open, I'm sure. "I...oh...

crap, Elly," I said her name and she didn't look at me.

Instead, she looked at the clock on the bookshelf. "I need to go. Pick me up tomorrow." With that, she got up and walked towards the stairs.

I sat with the open atlas on the floor and tried to see up her skirt as she climbed the basement steps.

And then I hated myself.

And then I had some gin.

And sure enough, self-loathing doesn't go away that easily.

So I thought that maybe I should have some more.

CHRIS

"Dude, you got anything to eat?"

I'm feeling wonderfully woozy. "You can check the fridge." Having a best friend means never having to accompany them when they offer to get food.

"Okay. Your mom home?"

"No. She wouldn't mind. You can check the cabinet, too."

Chris runs upstairs. "Hey! Get some Pringles or something for me, okay?" I'm not sure if he hears me or not, but it doesn't matter. He comes back down with a box of Fiddle Faddle and a carton of milk.

"Scott, dude, it sucks. Angela was waiting for me at Denny's and my mom made me paint my sister's room."

"When was this?"

"Last night. I was one mushroom-cloud-laying moth-
erfucker."

"Sucks." Sounded like *thucks*. Mmm...Fiddle Faddle.

"I was like the fucking *Guns of Navarone*."

"The what?"

"*Guns of Navarone*. It's a movie." Chris is patronizing
when it comes to movies.

"Oh. Couldn't the painting wait?"

"No. I'd put it off, for, like two months. And my dad
was all, *If you don't do it, I'm taking your car away and im-
pounding it*."

"Oh."

"I got pink paint all over my Dave Matthews shirt."
Chris whines and drinks from the carton.

"Dude, you have, like, fifteen of those."

"Two."

"Fifteen, two, whatever. Too many." Dave Matthews,
my ass.

"Hey, I don't make fun of that Bones Brigade piece of
shit you never take off."

"Hey! This jacket is a quality piece of counter-culture.
A fine specimen of my clearly un-mainstream beliefs."
I'm not completely serious. It's something I found in the
attic. I just forget to take it off. Sometimes for days.

"Whatever, dude. It's an over-glorified skating jacket
and you don't even skate."

"I don't have to skate to appreciate the beauty of the
Bones Brigade."

"Uh." Chris is unimpressed.

Welcome to an impasse.

"Okay. Point taken. Can I have that?" I reach for the Fiddle Faddle. Chris passes the box into my outstretched palm and picks up a Rubik's Cube on the TV tray next to the couch.

"There's a show in the city on Sunday. All ages and I hear the guitarist is quite ridiculous." Chris is always finding ridiculous guitarists.

"How much are the tickets?" Ridiculous guitarists usually mean a pretty good time. I like good times.

"I dunno. Twelve bucks? Ten?"

Reasonable. "Okay. Can you drive?"

Pause.

"You can actually come? Now there's a surprise." I'd like you all to meet a very bitter Chris.

"What? I don't get paid till Thursday. I've got the money for the ticket, but I need an oil change and I don't—"

Chris interrupts. "You can *actually* go?" He really is bitter. I've passed up a month of shows and several weeks of our ongoing Super Mario Tournament.

"Yeah. "

"And you don't want to bring Elly?" He is mocking me.

"I dunno. I guess not. I don't think she'd want to."

"Oh. Good. 'Cause I only have two tickets."

"You already bought them?"

"My mom did. I just have to pay her back."

"When?"

"Last week."

"And you're asking me now?"

"Yeah, Angela didn't want to."

"Oh." In my absence, the girlfriend has taken over. My turn to mock him. "Do you even like her?"

"I dunno."

"Dude, she makes you buy shit, like flowers. She actually *demands* that you buy her flowers. What is that?"

"You don't get Elly anything?"

"She's not my girlfriend."

"You just tapping that for free?"

Tapping? Where is he from? "No tapping."

"Bullshit, man. Bullshit." He puts the Rubik's Cube down and turns on the TV and the Nintendo and tosses me a controller. "She's all over the place. You spend way too much time with her to not have."

"I'm telling you." I shake my head.

"That's just sad, then."

"No kidding."

BECOMING SPECTACULAR

"I think the big problem today is that people don't spend enough time on self reflection." I can see my breath, so I make sure to enunciate *reflection*. RE-FLEC-T-I-OOOOOOOOOOO-N. I fail at making a smoke ring.

"I can see that." Elly's breath puffs back towards her, but her head is down, so she doesn't notice it. I'm strange, because I count the days we do this. Every day after school. Like clockwork. And at eleven a.m. on weekends. Like clockwork. This is our fifth week.

What are we doing? We're sitting on a wall in the community park with our feet dangling over a stream.

"I mean, we have a society full of people who take anti-depressants because they don't know why they're sad—but they never bother to find out what's making them so sad. There's so much there that's so scary sometimes."

"Tell me about it."

"But you know, right? You see it."

"I do. But they don't know how to fix it. That's the way everything is. Quick fix. That's why everything is so disposable."

I nod and look down at my shoes. Then I look at her out of the corner of my eye. I wagered to myself that my arms would feel nice around her hunched shoulders.

"I wonder when this world got so fucking fun." I spit to make my point.

"It's always been that way."

Another nod and my gaze drifts back towards down.

"Can I ask you a question, Scott?"

"Yeah. "

"When'd you start?"

"Start what?"

She nudges the Poland Spring bottle that sits between us. "Drinking." The word sounds dirty.

"I dunno." Two years, eight months. Three weeks, ten days. Four hours. Eight minutes. Forty-six seconds. The universe has been expanding at an infinitesimal rate ever since.

"Okay..."

"Ninth grade?"

"See? Not so hard."

"Meh. It's not something I think about." Two years, eight months. Three weeks, ten days. Four hours. Nine minutes. Seventeen seconds. Another Milky Way is born. I pick up the bottle and toast to my big bang. "You see, Elly, as every good liquor aficionado," I pause and laugh at myself, "knows, it's not how long. It's how much."

"Uh, right."

"You shoulda met me in middle school." Heh, heh. Snort, snort.

"I bet you looked exactly the same." My ego winces.

"Oh man, I wouldn't talk to *anyone*, let alone *girls*." Girls? Ew! Cooties!

"You seemed just fine when I met you."

"You didn't leave me much choice, now, did you?"

"Hey, here's a weird question. Did I kiss you?"

"Uh, Yep." One month, one week, four days, seventeen hours, sixteen minutes, nine seconds. Memory like a trap.

"Wow...I don't even remember that." Oh. Never mind.

"Yeah, it happened."

"How do you even remember that? How much did you drink?"

"I have a liver of steel. I am infallible."

"Oh, right, I forgot." She takes a drink now, too.

"No, but seriously. I was so afraid of people in middle school. People used to think I was this little snob 'cause I wouldn't talk. It was just 'cause I was afraid of people."

"So what happened?"

"The greatest thing. I met Chris."

"Eh." Elly doesn't like Chris. She thinks he's...*pretentious*. Or something.

"His older brother went to college and became, like, an absolute drunk. And we thought he was so cool. Oh, man. 'Cause he had a *bong* and shit. Like, when does a twelve-year-old get to see a *bong*? We didn't even know what it was, but he had to be all hush-hush about it, so of course we were awesome for having seen it. When does even a *high school* kid get to see a bong? I mean, seriously. That's what fables are made of. It was cool!"

"You have a weird definition of cool sometimes, you know that?"

"Eh. Anyway, Chris had this great idea that we try drinking. And where better than at my house?"

"'Cause your mom and dad are gone during the day."

"Yeah. Oh man, by six, I was, like, three sheets to the wind." Maybe I'm exaggerating a little. In the beginning, we thought it tasted like poison. So we only had a little.

"Seriously? Geez, what'd your mom say?"

"Capful of Scope and fifteen minutes convincing myself that I was in control and I was cool." Yeah, a little bit of exaggeration. But still. Never hurt anybody.

"I don't believe that."

"Seriously!" For the most part. Except for the whole being-absolutely-smashed part. Alcohol grows on you slowly. "I don't think my parents noticed. We added a little water to the gin we took. My dad drinks and has people over often enough that if we were careful, it was okay. I guess my mom just thought we were being…fourteen." Or maybe she just didn't want to know.

Elly is still holding the bottle with the cap off. "It just made happier."

"Happier?"

"Or happy at all."

"Oh." What do you say to that? Nothing.

Except *Oh.*

"Sorry." She puts the bottle down. Pass it around, pass it around. I put the cap back on.

"Don't be. I'm sorry."

"Not your fault."

"I know, but still."

"Let's talk about something else."

"Sorry."

"It's okay." We both look down, swinging our feel a little. I offer her the bottle and she takes it and looks at it for a second. Then she looks at me. "Can we get Chinese food to go with this?"

"Yeah."

Anything for you, dear.

A FEW WORDS FOR MY ADORING PUBLIC

I kick so much ass, it's almost unbelievable.

Look at me.

Seventeen years old. Writing this killer...poetry. God, I'm a girl. Maybe I'll start on stories. Maybe something about how man gets stuck as a cog in a vast international corporate machine.

Oh, wait. That's me, working at McDonalds.

About a superior race of aliens who show us the light of a...utopia...where girls are slaves and...no, back up there. That's what I was thinking about in the bathroom five minutes ago. Where scrawny retards like me rule the planet because of our vast and superior knowledge of... Columbian literature in translation. Hey, it could happen?

Now I know why Poe liked opium so much. Everyone needs a muse.

Hello, there, Mr. Beefeater.

Hello, Scott. It's a pleasure to make your acquaintance.

You have no idea.

Scott, you are in the prime of your life. You'll be on the cover of Rolling Stone *in no time. So tell the audience, what inspires you to write these incredible, breathtakingly human novels at such a young age?*

To tell the truth, I've always felt I had some sort of insight into the human condition that very few other humans have. I'm not afraid to say what most people are afraid to even recognize in themselves. They read my stuff and they identify, but they don't know why. That's the key to my brilliance. Self-awareness and honesty. I feel like people in this day and age are just not self-reflective enough to know themselves. I do it *for* them.

You don't say.

I do.

That's fascinating. How are you dealing with this international literary stardom?

I'm keeping it real.

No, not keeping it real. That's what everyone says. Scratch that.

I'm staying me.

No, too humble.

Trying my hardest not to forget where I come from.

Excellent. I'm still Scotty from the block. Good answer. Now, I read somewhere once that at the beginning of his career, Robin Williams told something different about his family history to everyone. Maybe I'll do the same.

So tell us, Scott. What was it like growing up? What drew you to writing?

Well, my father had a master's degree in...Botanical Sciences from...Oxford. And my mother is an internationally revered...chef. I'm sure you've heard of her. She goes by the name Wolfgang Puck. Yup, that guy is just a stand-in. She is the brilliance behind him.

That's fascinating.

Growing up in such a diverse household. What with my father constantly having big money over for dinner—he...ran a school for...estate gardening...and people like the Kennedy's were constantly in his debt for having such…awesome lawns—and my mother always opening restaurants and having people like…Liberace and Michael Jackson over. No, he seemed like a nice guy. Didn't touch me at all. Anyway, growing up in an environment like that, I had a lot to draw from and felt as if I had a lot to say to the rest of the world.

I can imagine. What was school like for you?

Well, we moved around a lot, you know, because of my mom's amazing cooking. So I put a lot of time into my writing. I was a bit of a recluse. You know how it goes. Never popular—afraid to talk to girls.

You? Afraid to talk to girls?

Yeah! Can you believe it! I would get so nervous. I would absolutely choke.

Hardly. You're a witty and charming individual.

I know. Now I am. Have you met my girlfriend, Elly?

No, but we've seen tabloid pictures of the two of you.

A knockout, right?

She really is.

She really, truly understands me. She makes me feel like I'm the only person in the world when I'm around her. She's great.

So tell us, what's your next work going to be about?

I'm working on a sort of pseudo-fiction. It sounds trite, but really, it's quite good. About a frustrated seventeen-year-old boy.

It's quite daring to go into such an over-saturated genre.

Yes, but I think I can pull it off.

What an enviable status you've achieved in life.

I really owe it all to God for my talent. I can't really say that what I create is mine. It comes from a higher power.

It's been really great talking to you, Scott, and it looks like we're almost out of gin. But just one thing: This is kind of funny, because we have reports here that your mother has her GED and works part time at the library and your father has an associate's degree in...business...and works at...a high school. As a janitor. And they're not so much married as two old people who co-exist with you. Elly doesn't even begin to think of you as a male and when you showed your poetry to your mother, she laughed at you for a week straight for using the words "you are like a budding flower/ who hasn't budded yet."

Oh, that's just what I tell some interviewers. You know, to mix it up. But I told you guys the truth. What, 'cause you're *Rolling Stone* and all. Trust me. I am a creative individual, you know, and sometimes I really like to have my privacy. That's my way of having privacy.

We have your mother here to confirm it.

Oh, shit.

I live in your liquor cabinet, Scott. I know all.

I guess there's no use denying that I drink, then?

Have a swig, Scotty boy. You're not going anywhere for a while.

SO

She looked like someone had her on an invisible choke

chain. Everything that came out of her mouth sounded like a secret.

"So, you're a friend of Elly's?"

"Yes, ma'am."

"She's in the bathroom fixing herself up. She'll be out in a minute. Have a seat. Do you want some iced tea?" She said this almost inaudibly.

"I'm okay. Thank you, though."

She continued to stand where she had stopped when she asked me to come in.

"I can wait here." I offered so that maybe she could go back to what she was doing. That, and she made me feel like the world was watching me.

She nodded and smiled and then said something about me being nice.

"Wha...?" I took a step closer

"That's nice. You said your name was Matt?"

"Oh. No. Scott."

"That's nice. Well, I had better get back to that kitchen."

"It was nice meeting you."

She turned around and shuffled a few steps towards the doorway she'd come in from. Then she turned back to me.

"Scott. What class are you in?"

"Class? Oh, junior."

"That's nice."

"Yeah. Not a bad class."

"That's nice. Do you want to go to college?"

"I'm thinking about it."

"That's nice."

I laughed uncomfortably. "We'll see."

"Do you do *well* in school?" She nodded as she said *well* as if to signify that *well* was a word I might not understand.

"I do. . ." I thought for a moment, "...well."

"That's nice. Your parents must be proud."

"Not *that* well." I smiled again. Uncomfortably. So did she. A fake smile.

"I'll go check on Elly."

Mother *exeunt*.

I stood in the foyer for a bit, waiting. Then Elly emerged from a room off the hall, walking quickly.

"We're out," she said as she walked past me and out the door.

I looked behind me at the empty foyer and hallway.

"Have a nice afternoon!" I called into the empty space and waited for a reply.

When the screen door hit the door frame a moment later, I looked out and saw Elly, already halfway to my car. I turned and left as well.

RIKI-OH!

"I can't believe I came over here to watch this." Elly has placed herself in the Laz-E-Boy next to the couch. I have placed myself on the couch. Near the Laz-E-Boy. So close. So far.

"So cool, Elly."

She studies the screen for a minute.

"This is so bad. Look at that! That guy just punched that guy's stomach and it looked like he punched a papier-mâché balloon! And all that tomato juice came out! He doesn't even have internal organs! That's horrible special effects!"

"That's exactly what's so wonderful about it."

"I don't think I get it."

"Sorry."

"Meh. I like hanging out. Even if it's for a bad movie."

"Bad in a good way, I swear."

"I'll take your word on that."

"You really want to see bad? I should get out *Evil Dead*."

"Uh."

"Well, I won't go overkill. Next time. But you *have* to see it."

She laughs and looks at me with an enormous. Heart melting. Smile.

"You're a nut job. Adorable. But a nut job."

Adorable. I'm adorable. I have the ability to be adored.

"I do what I can."

"And you do okay."

She musses my hair.

Then there is silence. We both stare straight ahead. I peek to the side. The minute she moves her head, I stare back at the TV. Nope, no one here 'cept us chickens looking at the TV and not looking at you like a sick little puppy. 'Cause I'm not. At all.

One more peek won't hurt.

"Maybe we'll watch *Evil Dead* on Thursday." She relents aloud, apparently to some argument she was having in her head.

Hmm...Thursday? Oh, crap.

"Can't."

She looks up. "What?"

"I promised Chris I'd go with him to the city."

"Oh." Disappointment.

"Sorry. We planned it a while ago."

"What're you gonna do?"

"See a band."

"Which one?"

"Some band Chris likes. Psychedelic Breakfast?"

"Oh."

"He only had two tickets. Otherwise..."

"No, it's cool. I was just curious."

"You can come over anyway. I'm sure my mom would let you watch it."

"That's okay. I'll wait. How about Saturday?"

"Um, okay."

Her face lights up. "Great. I got this guy to buy me some White Zin."

"Great. "

She pauses for a minute. "Do you know what Saturday is?"

"The weekend?"

She eyes me.

And this, Ladies and Gentlemen, is why we should just be going out.

MORTAL KOMBAT

Today is Elly's seventeenth birthday. It's a rainy Saturday. I pick her up at eleven and take her to a diner in town for breakfast. We laugh about the couple sitting behind her. I'm convinced they're breaking up because the girl is crying and the guy keeps making like he's gonna put on his jacket and run.

I buy her chocolate chip pancakes and cheese fries. I prefer black coffee and a cherry blintz. She asks the waitress for a job application. I make her smile when I tell her about my fantasy of watching the end of the world from a lawn chair on a plateau and a CamelBak of Coors.

We make it to the bottle of White Zinfandel in my car at around four p.m. after walking around downtown. She lets me smoke and I let her wear my sweatshirt because it's chilly. She has no other plans for the day. Just me. Just her. So we sit in my car parked in my driveway and drink.

At 5:30, I get a phone call and my mother comes outside to tell me that I should come inside and answer it. It's Chris. He says there is a party tonight. Dress like a video game character and drinks are free. Elly is game. I am game. Party starts at ten.

Elly borrows a green t-shirt from me and is Frogger. I

put on a white shirt and say I am Pong. Some people are more creative. We just want free booze.

When we arrive, I lose Elly and Chris almost immediately. I end up, several hours later, half asleep in a corner, listening to a thin, freckled boy talk about the superiority of Ol' Dirty Bastard over most other musicians. Ever. I feel like Kevin Spacey looks after he's been shot in the head at the end of *American Beauty*. I probably wouldn't mind my brains decorating the walls, either. It is when Freckle-Face begins explaining how a forty of Old English arrived in his white, white hands that a shorter, darker-haired, but equally pale boy arrives in front of me.

"You're Scott?"

"Yeah. "

"Your girlfriend wants five minutes and then she wants to go home."

Not my girlfriend. I stand up. "Where is she?"

"Bathroom, dude."

"Over there?" I point where I was lead to believe it was.

"Yeah. She's not done yet, though."

"Jesus."

I say this because I know. Because I know what is about to happen. Because it's her birthday. Because of Ol' Dirty Bastard. Because I'm in one of those moods. I open the bathroom door without knocking. The tub is empty. Except for Elly. And Chris. Elly toasts me from the bathtub with a shampoo bottle. From under Chris. "Hey there, sailor."

"Scott—Christ, knock." Chris sits back in the tub and Elly sits up, grabbing for her shirt—my shirt—from the toilet seat and pulling the bottom of her skirt away from her navel. I'm standing, looking down at both of them. I am about to burst.

"I—fuckin'—" I stop myself from apologizing and look at Chris. He stands up and pulls up his pants. He exhales and gives me a guilty grin. *Got her.*

I envision myself throwing a punch which lands squarely on his nose. I envision an all-out brawl. I envision myself standing atop Chris and Elly cowering in the bathtub, still half-naked. I taste blood in my mouth and victory in my pants.

I stay where I am.

Chris steps out of the tub. "I think we're done here. It's late, we should go."

Snap.

"Shut up." I half-push, half-punch him in the shoulder. He stumbles back and almost trips over the toilet. He blinks. I watch him take a step forward and punch me in the jaw. My head cracks against the bathroom wall and I let myself slide to the floor. Elly whimpers loudly.

"I'll find my own ride, thanks." He walks out and leaves the door open.

I rub the left side of my face and look at Elly. She doesn't look up.

"Whore." I get up and walk out.

Elly ends up in the car next to me. I suppose she

doesn't have another choice, but I don't remember her getting in. I realize she's there when we're already half-way home.

"I'm sorry." She says this so that I can only barely hear her over the wipers. I don't say anything. "Scott?"

"What?" My voice sounds colder than I intend it to be. But that's what happens when you say things through your teeth.

"It's silly—"

I cut her off. "What's silly, Elly? What's silly?"

"You shouldn't—"

"I shouldn't what? I shouldn't hit people? No, you're right, I shouldn't fucking hit people. No one should fucking hit anyone, Elly. And if they do, other people shouldn't stay around for it." I am unusually cruel.

"Are you *blaming*—"

"Fuck you, Elly. Fuck you. Happy fucking birthday. I hope you fucking enjoyed it. I sure did. But you must tell me, Elly. Will you sleep with my friends on *my* birthday, too? Because I'm beginning to think you're doing this as a favor to me. I really am."

"Scott, I don't—"

"How many bathtubs, bedrooms, cars and sofas do I get to pull you off of, Elly? I'm just the friend who puts up with it, right? None of *them* would put up with it. 'Cause I'm a fucking doormat. Do you even use a condom? Do I have to drive you to Planned Parenthood later, too, or some shit? What the fuck do you think you're doing?"

She is silent. I hit the wheel with my palm and bite my

lip. Then, there are only the wipers again. And my anger.

She speaks again after I turn onto her street. "I was gonna ask." She pauses to see if I will yell. I say nothing and wait for her to continue. "Can I stay with you tonight?"

I say nothing. I continue to drive up the block.

"Scott, listen."

My best friend just punched me, Elly.

I stop in front of her house and put the car in park. She does not get out. She turns to face me. She swims in my jacket and t-shirt.

"I thought maybe so I won't—"

You just slept with my best friend, Elly.

"Get out." I say this quietly. She looks at me and I hear her exhale. Her face distorts in disgust.

"Get your head out of your ass." She gets out and slams the door. I watch her walk across the lawn to her darkened house. I only pull away when I see her parents' bedroom light go on. If she doesn't hate me, I do.

Asshole.

ANOTHER RAINY NIGHT

Only in America would we call over-eating a sport. They had shrimp-eating on ESPN. Large guys lined up in a hall in Alaska, eating shrimp. The guy who came in second did so by dipping each shrimp into a special sauce. He said it helped his digestion. The guy who won ate four and a half pounds of shrimp. No special sauce.

The entire affair inspired me to put down my root beer Popsicle in an empty glass and watch it melt. I turned off the TV and watched the clock. Nine p.m. on a Sunday night. Ah, where have the days of my carefree youth gone? I was drunk at three o'clock and sober by six. Perhaps I needed a night cap. A big fucking night cap. I decided a trip to the basement was in order as soon as my Popsicle was melted. Perhaps it would mix well with something.

Elly hadn't come by. She hadn't called. I'd spent the day jerking off to internet porn and reading *Truman*. Earlier in the day, I'd had a few shots of Citron and had accompanied my father to Sears. Because Citron is in order when it comes to my father. He likes to play Disneyland Dad. Never home during the week. Your best friend on weekends. And of course he decided to have a talk on the way to Sears.

"Scooter." Yes, he called me Scooter. "Scooter," he said, "I don't want to pry because I leave well enough alone and for the most part, you seem well enough."

Okay... "Thanks, Dad."

"But your mother says she thinks you've been getting into trouble with that girl, Elly."

"Dad..." Please, don't go there.

"Now, I know boys will be boys, and all that crapola, but we just wanted to make sure you were okay."

"I'm okay, dad."

"Because if I were your age, I'd be more than just

friends with that girl, if you know what I mean." He chuckled deeply. "She's a good-looking girl, Scooter. But be careful. If there's any way your mother and I can help, please let us know."

He means condoms. Oh my God, he's talking about condoms. "Okay, dad."

"And listen, one more thing."

Aw, Christ. "Yeah, dad?"

"I'm not telling your mother about your little habit. But for Chrissake, you smell like last call. So think about it, okay? I don't want to have this talk with you again."

"Uh…" Under the guise of looking out the window, I discretely exhaled onto my arm and tried to catch a whiff of my own breath. Was it that strong? The Scope wasn't working?

"Smoking, Scooter. Quit it. Who even gets those cancer sticks for you? You want to end up like Grandpa with a respirator and tubes all over you before you die? Don't be stubborn. I don't want to outlive my kid, okay?"

Phew. "Okay, dad."

"Someday you're going to have kids and they're going to be just like you. And only then will you realize how little you know. Until then, just give your old man the benefit of the doubt. I'm just doing my job. For once, try not to be stubborn."

"You got it, dad."

"I knew you'd listen. Thanks."

And there I was, a bucket-of-screws-and-a-Marlboro

later, waiting for the thing that surpassed the prospect of sex with Elly and nicotine. It was almost time to even up.

I decided the liquor would melt the rest of the Popsicle, so I went downstairs to replace *Truman* and obtain a little more sanity.

Tonight's adventure was tequila. Root beer Popsicle and tequila. Breakfast of champions. I sat down by the bookcase with, appropriately, a Vonnegut and enjoyed six ounces of two liquids that I would never mix again. By my estimates, I was drooling on the floor by page fifteen.

Hi Ho.

My mother found me there around one-thirty in the morning.

"Scott, I've been looking everywhere for you."

"Sorry mom, I think I fell..."

"There's a phone call for you. Can you *please* tell your friends to call no later than eleven? I have work in the morning."

I got up. "Who is it?"

"It sounds like Elly."

I picked her up outside of the library. She was wet and her hair was matted against her head. She was sobbing.

"Scott," She said between sobs when she got into the car, "Thank you, and tell your mom I'm sorry for waking her up." That's the least of my worries.

"It's okay. Don't worry. What happened to you?"

"She sounded." Sob. "Upset." Deep Inhale. "She said

it was late."

"It's okay, she'll live. What happened?"

"So tell her I didn't mean for it." She broke into tears.

"Elly, don't worry! What happened to you?"

"And I won't call this late again, I promise. I'm sorry."

"Elly! Stop being sorry! What happened?"

"I just needed to leave."

"Leave? Leave what? What happened?" She's dancing around something. I'm so lost.

"I needed to go for a walk."

"It's raining outside, Elly! What happened?" What happened? What happened? How many times do I have to say it?

"I couldn't stay, I needed to leave for a while."

"Okay. Do you want me to take you somewhere?" Please. Tell me what I can do. I don't know.

"I just needed to dry off for a while."

"Elly! What happened? Why did you leave? Tell me *something!*" Anything.

"I don't need help, I just need to be dry and quiet for a while." She put her forehead against my shoulder. I raised my hand and patted her head lightly, not knowing what else to do. Sticky.

Sticky?

"Elly, what's..." I turned on the light. *Jesus.* "Elly, you're bleeding." So that's what happened.

"I'm sorry."

I almost laughed. "Don't be sorry. You're bleeding!

Do you need a doctor?"

"No. It'll be okay." Concussion? God, head wound. Totally not prepared for this.

"It's your head! Are you sure? Who did this?"

She broke into heavy sobs and buried her face in my sweatshirt and mumbled something.

"I...can't...hear you." I tried to lift her face up carefully. She was so ugly when she was crying. She sniffed violently and wiped her eyes on her sleeve.

"I forgot to clean..." she broke into heavy sobs again.

"You forgot to clean what?" Like pulling teeth. I want to *do* something. Help her. Like kill whoever did this to her.

Sob. "The living room."

"The *living room?*" What?

"I was supposed to yesterday and—" She rendered herself inaudible again.

"Elly, I can't hear you. You're mumbling."

"I'm sorry!" she wiped her nose on the wrist of her rugby shirt. I opened the glove compartment and handed her some napkins.

"Use these."

Sniffle. "Thank you."

"Now, you forgot to clean the living room?"

"I was supposed to and I didn't. All last week."

She was calming down a little, now hiccoughing.

"And what happened?"

"He got so upset. And he kept telling me, too."

"Who? Your dad?"

She nodded and blew her nose.

"Your *Dad* did this?" Oh God. I could kill him. Beautiful Elly. I could kill him.

"Scott, you can't tell anybody. I didn't mean to—" She broke into sobs again. I didn't know what to do. We should tell someone. I should call the cops. This girl is bleeding. Someone tell me what to do! This isn't right! He should be arrested! Imprisoned! Shot! Hung! Lynched!

But, instead, I drove to my house. On the way, I put this together: living room—dirty—father—whiskey—trip—rawhide—daughter—brass reading lamp.

She made a request for the basement.

As she fell asleep on the couch, the remainder of the Tequila dangling in her pink fingers, she limply toasted me. "Like father, like daughter."

I could only say one thing: "You could never be like him."

How thoughtful.

SYNCHRONICITY

I fucking hate my life.

I hate myself. And my life.

I can't stand lying on this couch because it means I have to be in my goddamned body. I hate my body. I need to get out. Get out. Get the *fuck* out. How can I get out? Maybe I can go run. Or lift weights. Or eat? I could stand to gain a few pounds. Except my stomach is flabby. I'm a skinny kid with a flabby stomach. How long does it take to get a six pack? Too long, probably.

God, my life sucks. No one cares about me or anything I do. I could blow something up. Then maybe someone would care. It's too late for me to do something good with my life. My grades suck. I have no friends. Except Chris. But he's off fucking Angela. Why does he get ass? I need some ass. Oh, and Elly. But she's probably off fucking…anyone but me. I'm such a fucking loser. In this fucking jacket watching this fucking TV. I can't stand to listen to it anymore. Mute. Mute. Mute. Fuck you, TV. Care about me!

Someone? Anyone?

Please?

Maybe I can kill myself.

But how do I kill myself?

I could hang myself out the window. But that means suffocating. I hear it's quite a high when your brain has no oxygen. Like auto-asphyxiation without the reviving part. Too gross, though.

No guns, so I can't shoot myself in the mouth. Plus, what if I pull what that guy in *Fight Club* pulled? No holes in my neck for me, thank you. I want my mother to be able to have an open casket.

Maybe I'll take pills. Lots of pills. Tylenol? No…if you survive from Tylenol, your liver is still shot. I need my liver if I survive so I can drink myself to death later in life. Maybe Motrin then. I wonder what Motrin does to your insides. Should I run with plain old aspirin? Maybe I've still got some of that stuff they gave me when I had mono...what was it? Codeine. God, that was good shit. Mix that with a whole bunch of Jack and I'll be dead within the hour.

Or maybe I'll just lie here. Watch *Behind the Music*. Maybe if I do that with my eyes closed and an empty aspirin bottle in my hand, then maybe someone will *think* I tried to commit suicide. Then the police will come and Elly will stop fucking whoever she's fucking and Chris will leave Angela and my mom will come home from work and stroke my arm and tell me it's okay. God, I'm a pussy. Will they pump my stomach? Elly says they give you charcoal. I wonder what that tastes like. Is it gritty? Is it worth it?

God, I fucking hate my life. And myself. No one could even begin to like me. Of course they don't. I'm pale and have these fucking glasses and I say the *weirdest* shit. It always seems okay in my head, but then I end up being so goddamned weird and I *know* I'm being weird, but I can't stop it from happening. Jesus Christ, Scott! Why don't you just block your exhaust pipe and be done with it!

That's it...I'll find a gym sock and block the exhaust pipe. How ironic! I fucking hate gym. Of course it would be the thing that would kill me. Stupid high school gym. Fuckers.

Oh, wait, I love this video. Man, I love Nirvana. He was such a fuckhead for killing himself. He actually had talent. Unlike me. I'm just a talentless loser. Who can't get a girl.

Oh Christ. If I kill myself, it would severely inhibit my

ability to watch this video. And this is a good freaking video. Look at that. He's a god. I can't die and not be able to watch this video.

That just won't do.

BONES BRIGADE

I'm seventeen. I'm in love. I have a Bones Brigade jacket. Damn, I'm cool.

What I didn't tell you about Elly is this:

I think she's beautiful. She's short and she's beautiful. She has crooked bottom teeth and she's beautiful. And I want, with all my heart, to be close enough to smell her.

When I'm combing my hair, I'm awesome. I'm James Dean. I'm a rebel without a cause. I'm Dirty Harry. I'm gonna rock. I'm gonna roll. I give myself a sideways smile.

Tonight, my car is a Jaguar. My earring is a diamond. My brother is Sid Vicious. And I'm going out with Jessica Rabbit. Depeche Mode writes my incidental music.

I'll write a poem. About how she wears sweatshirts and skirts and sneakers. And about those soda-can tabs she wears around her neck that she told me spell out the name of her dog. Or maybe later. Because we've got a date with cheap Italian food and an evening with the *Evil Dead* trilogy. I'm rolling out. To pick up my girl, who's not really, but kind of cos she spends everyday at my house and you know she *wants me woo!*

"Scott?"

"Mom! I'm on my way to pick up Elly."

"Can I talk to you for a second?"

"I'm really in a rush, mom. I'm late picking her up."

"Scott, you smell like the Old Spice factory blew up in your room."

"You think it's too much?"

"Yes. And considering the fact that you're grounded, it's *much* too much."

FOUR

There are certain times in your life when you realize that there is some serious mis-wiring in your brain. Like when you drink and drive, for instance.

Not only does drinking severely impair your judgment and reaction time when driving. In my case, it also gives me every right to be an asshole. In my head.

On Tuesday night, my mom received a report card populated mostly by C's and maybe one or two or five D's. We fought. She took my keys. I had spares. I took my car on a speed rampage through town. In freezing rain. Just me, Metallica and the Beefeater. And of course I was going to get away with it. Seventeen is equivalent to immortal. Death and police play no part in my little world of self-righteousness.

So when a dark blue Ford Taurus skidded into the back of my car at a relatively low speed at a stop light at around midnight-ish, I did the most logical thing a half-cut immortal could think of.

I took a rusted nine-iron I happened to have out of my trunk and beat the shit out of the culprit car's bumper.

PHONE TAG

1:31 a.m.

"Hi. You've reached Rich, Samantha and Eleanor. Please leave a message after the beep and we'll get back to you."

Beeeeeeeeeeeeeep.

"Elly? You there? It's me, Scott. Please, please, please, please pick up. Listen, Something really weird happened and I'm at the *police station* in town. I'm really sorry it's so late, but if you could maybe borrow your dad's car or something and come bail me out, I'd really owe you. This is just a little thing. You see, this guy hit my car and I got a little overexcited—but the guy didn't press charges or anything. He didn't have a licence. Phew, right? But you see, I was kind of drun…"

"Hello?" A sleepy voice picked up on the line, shutting off the answering machine.

"Hi. I'm really sorry. Is Elly there?"

"Who the *fuck* is this?"

"This is Scott. Elly—"

"Who the *hell* is Scott? What do you want?"

"I'm Elly's friend."

The receiver is covered. Muffled voices. *What is it?*
Do you know a Scott? Yes, Elly has a friend. Well, he's on the
phone. It's two a.m. I know, what a punk. He seems like a nice
boy. He's calling at two o'clock in the morning—what the hell
do you know?

"Scott?"

"Yes, sir?"

"Elly is in bed."

"Sir, I'm really sorry, but can you get her? She won't—"

"Scott, you realize it's two o'clock in the morning."

"Yessir. "

"Scott, you realize that right now I'd beat the living
shit out of you if you were in front of me."

"Sir—"

"Don't *sir* me."

"I understand it's late, but I'm at the police station
downtown and this is my one phone call—" Please...
Click.

2:13 a.m.

"Scott's Line. Leave one."

Beeeeeep.

"Scott, it's Elly. Listen, uh, first of all, I'm sorry about
not being home. I know we had plans... I'm really sorry for
not calling or anything before this. I'll make it up to you.
But listen, I'm in Reddington. I don't know if you know
where that is, but I need to be picked up. I'm at the Seven-
eleven in Reddington. You remember Dan from that...ah,

fuck it. I can't get home. He left me here. My parents don't know I left. Please, please, please, pick up. Oh god." *Click.*

TYPE TWO

I've come to the conclusion that there are several types of phone calls.

There are the kinds that you wait by the phone for. There are the ones that make your heart race because they're unexpectedly good. There are the kinds where your voice stays low because you're talking about something that is of a certain intrigue. Then there are the kinds that you don't pick up because you know it's something you don't want to deal with. There are the kinds where you pick up like an idiot because you thought it was going to be unexpectedly good. There are the kinds that ring and you pick up because you're sure nothing else could go wrong that day. And there are the kinds that you pick up, but you don't say anything.

"Scott. Is there something you need to tell me?"

My mom got one of those last ones from Elly's mom.

"No, mom. Why?"

"Where were you last night?"

Air gets caught in my throat.

"I can explain."

"First, I'd like your car keys."

And she hadn't even gotten my father involved yet.

GUIDANCE

"Scott, I'm sure you know why you're here."

"I think so." Everyone knows. Chris is calling me Ti-ger Woods. So is my history teacher.

"I think there is something going on at home with Elly and she will not talk to us. Now, I feel as if it's the school's responsibility to protect children, to a certain extent, from any situations that cause them serious harm. As her coun-selor, I personally feel as if what she is not telling us could lead her to be in harm's way, or even harm herself. She has mentioned you in several of our sessions and it seems to me that you mean a lot to her. I want to know if you would be willing to help us out."

Surprise, surprise...

"Sure, I suppose. Elly said that?" Also a surprise.

"She mentions you frequently. She thinks a lot of you."

"Oh. That's funny." I am intrigued. Tell me more.

"It's funny?"

"No, I mean, I was just thinking. No, it's fine. What do you want?"

"Several of her teachers think there is something go-ing on at home. I am inclined to agree. She is absent fre-quently and I don't need to mention how she looks."

"No, ma'am." I've been friends with Elly for two marking periods. I'm the last person you need to men-tion this to.

"So, if Elly agrees and you don't feel as if you'd be betraying anything, I'd like you to come in once in a while. I think, whether you know it or not, you mean a lot to her and you can help her."

To tell the truth, I honestly couldn't see how I could help Elly. When presented with the self-inflicted responsibility to do something, I did the only thing that seemed to have any effect—albeit temporary—on the situation. I got her drunk. It's, sometimes, what she asked for, and others, what I saw as a remedy. Nothing else was within my power, as far as I could see.

"I'd like to help if I can, I guess."

"That's nice of you, Scott. I just have one question for you before we begin."

"Yes?"

"It says here...this last weekend..." She shuffled through some papers.

Oh, crap.

"It says here...that you were arrested for a DUI...and assault? Your parents informed the school. They wanted to know if we had any counseling programs available to students."

Gulp. "Yes, ma'am."

"The school would also like it, aside from your helping us with Elly, for you to attend a sort of alcohol abuse program we've set up here. I can be your counselor, too, if you like. I've told your parents about this program and..." More shuffling of papers, "...an off-site anger management program recommended by the school."

"Is it required?"

"It's not required, but your parents requested it and the school strongly recommends it. Perhaps you can take it up with them."

"I'll talk to them."

"Good. Are things at home okay for you, Scott? As I said before, this behavior is a bit surprising."

Dad sleeps on the couch. Girl with brass reading-lamp gashes in head. Nothing that ignoring can't fix. "It's fine."

"One last question before I let you go, Scott."

I nodded, the ball in my stomach expanding to my esophagus.

"Is Elly involved in any of this? For the most part, your records would lead us to believe that you are a good kid, so this was something of a surprise to me. However, your grades have gone down significantly this marking period. I am hoping that these few months are going to be an isolated and nonrecurring incident—you know, all this does affect your chances of getting into a good school."

I nod again, the scope of everything grasping me at my neck, making it very difficult, it seemed, for me to take in oxygen. "I know, ma'am."

"I also wanted to know if, perhaps, Elly might need this kind of treatment as well. Would she benefit from it?"

And the dilemma presents itself. I choose.

"I don't believe so, ma'am."

Ever have a rock in your stomach that stretches it down to the floor?

I saw Elly in the hall a few minutes after my session.
"What happened yesterday? I couldn't find you." Not
that her scattered attendance merited surprise.
"I went for a walk. I didn't feel like coming to school."
"You missed the French exam."
"Maybe I won't come tomorrow then, either." Good
thinking.
"I'll tell Madame you're sick."
"What do I have this time?"
"TB. They had to ship you to an iron lung."
"If only."
"I've got some vodka with me."
"You have no idea how much I missed you."

SUPER-SIZED LIFE

Alarm clock blaring.
Unsatisfactory life
Six-fucking-a.m.
Working mornings, nights and afternoons
I've measured out my life with...

Scene:
Red-eyed Mother in bathrobe holding car keys, coffee
cup. Pastel on canvas. Blue period.

Enter SON.
SON: Gee, Mom. Why are you coming in the front

door so early?

MOTHER: (*closing front door softly behind her, turns around, startled at son's presence*) Scott! What are you doing up?

SON: Golly, mom, it's the time I usually get up to start another rewarding Saturday as an employee of the McDonald's corporation.

MOTHER: I just had to go out and pick up something.

Awkward silence between MOTHER and SON

There are several ways you can take your mother coming in your front door at six a.m. wearing her bathrobe and carrying car keys and a cup of 7-11 coffee. Lucky for me, I don't get to choose.

"Have you seen your father?"

"No."

"He's not here."

"I dunno, mom."

"He didn't come home last night."

"I dunno, mom. I just got up." I feel like I've done something wrong.

"When did you go to bed last night?"

"I dunno, mom."

"Was it after me?"

"Mom, I dunno. Probably like eleven? Twelve? I was reading..."

"You didn't sneak out, did you?"

"Mom! No!"

"Right. Sorry, honey. Can you get a ride to work?" She rushes past me into the kitchen.

"I suppose I could call Dan or something..."

"Please." She yells from the sink, banging the dishes around, mumbling to herself.

"I could always take my car...just for today..." Dishes drop and resonate in the aluminum sink. Footsteps to the doorway of the kitchen. She looks at me, seeing if I'm serious.

"I can't even begin to answer you. Do you want you... us...me...to get arrested *again.*" Salt on an open wound makes me back down. "Just get a ride, okay? I can't *deal* with your father *and* you right now." She walks back into the kitchen and slams some things around in the fridge. Drops something. I haven't moved.

"Right." I stay put. "Do you need anything? Like, while I'm at the shopping center anyway...at work?"

"No!" I hear her scooping something out of a bowl into the garbage. I decide to move. Towards the kitchen. Brave son takes steps out of comfortable ignorance.

"Mom...have *you* seen dad?"

"No." She continues to scrape the empty bowl into the garbage and then slams it into the sink. Ties a knot in the garbage bag and walks out the back door into the garage. Slamming of can lids. Slamming of back door. She turns on the radio. I turn on the blender.

She stops. And looks at me. I look back at her.

I lie. "I'm late." I feel absurd in my golden arches next to an empty running blender. She looks wild in her hair and robe.

"Aren't you going to get a ride with Dan?"

"I haven't called him."

"You know how to use the phone."

"Yeah. "

She nods at the blender. I look at it.

"Mom. Where were you?"

She walks over and shuts it off.

"I told you. I had to go out." She unplugs it, wraps the cord around. Puts it in the cabinet. Takes it out.

"Mom..."

"*What* is it, Scott?"

"We keep that out on the counter."

"I *know*."

"Mom." I put my arm over her hands. She shrinks. Her bed-head wilts.

"Just go to work." She puts her arms around me and squeezes me briefly. I stay still. She fixes my collar. She smiles. And cries. And I stand and stare. And she tells me I look just like him. My dad.

"Honey, have a good day, okay? You look just like your dad. That little cowlick. Oh..." She licks her hand and smooths the side of my head. And cries. And bites her lip. Her skin matches the whites of her eyes. The pinks.

Do I, next to a trash can of cheese and smelly wild rice, have the strength to force the moment to its crisis?

"Mom. He's not home?"

She gives an ugly, unhappy smile. "No. You should call for your ride."

"Can you drive me?"

"I'm a mess."

"I've got some time."

"You're late. I'd need a shower."

"You're just driving me to the shopping center."

"He's out with some *woman*." The footman hangs my coat back up. I blink. She shakes her head and runs past me into the hall. She yells back at me. "No, shh. I didn't say that. Everything is going to be okay. I'm probably just overreacting. You shouldn't see me like this. I have to go back to sleep. Or take a shower."

"A *woman*? What *woman*, mom?" What did you do? My mother is crazy. I walk into the hall.

She's arranging things in the coat closet. Stops to look at me. A sneer. "I drove around this morning looking for his car."

"Maybe he had too much. Stayed at Gary's. It happened once before. Stays out late... Friday night."

She approaches me quickly. She straightens my collar again. "It wasn't at Gary's."

"That doesn't mean it's a *woman*, mom. Dad *has* other friends. You're just so freaking paranoid." A slap stings my cheek on the sound of *para*.

"You shut the fuck up. Walk to work. Get out."

"Mom! You're insane!"

"Oh, *I'm* insane. I'm not taking out any golf clubs, am I? Shut up."

"Mom!"

"Listen, you have no appreciation of what *I* have done

for you. *I* go through *hell* so you can live in this *house*. In this *neighborhood*. With *that* man in my bed every night."

"On the couch, mom...and I don't even want to know about that. And it isn't what you think it is. He's probably just staying. Got drunk."

"You don't know him, Scott. He's just dear old dad to you, isn't he? I've had enough. Get out. Go to work."

This isn't fair. It's just not fair.

"This isn't fair! You don't do this to me. I have to deal with people. I have to work all day."

"What isn't fair?"

"This. This whole thing. You're not supposed to tell me this stuff."

"No, that's right. I'm sorry. I have to deal with this silently. Well, excuse me. I've put up with your shit. *I* can't deal with any of this anymore! It's not fair to *me*. *Me*, Scott."

She has spit collecting at the corners of her mouth and her face is twisted in some sort of rage. I want to sneak away.

"Fine. Okay. Leaving." I turn.

"Go stay with your father if you're going to be so ungrateful. Wherever the hell he is. Don't come back." I run through the hall so I can end what I say next with a slamming front door.

"Don't worry, mom. I won't."

Would you like fries with that?

THINGS FALL APART

Roald Dahl is weird. He's a weird, weird guy. And that's who I was reading when Elly knocked at my window. I had to put down his book to open the window just a crack with my index finger to my mouth.

"Shh. . . what?"

"Can I come in?"

"It's two o'clock in the morning, Elly. Is home okay?"

"Just let me in, please." She had been crying. I directed her around to the side door. When I let her in, she wandered past me towards my room. "Can I stay with you tonight?"

"Uh..." I left my jaw open for a second and then, perhaps out of good training, turned down the hall towards my parent's bedroom. She grabbed my shoulder.

"No. Don't tell them. It's okay. I'll just stay on your floor or something."

"Uh." What? Who? When?

"Don't be thirteen. Please? Just tonight. No one will know. I don't want pity or anything. I just want to sleep."

"Elly, it really isn't very good here right now..."

"Scott. . ." Puppy face. Red, glassy eyes and puppy face.

"Yeah, yeah. You can take the bed, though. I'll go on the couch in the basement or something." Such a gentleman for being seventeen.

"No, it's okay. I just need a blanket on the floor."

"Oh. Okay. Would you rather take the couch in the

basement or something?"

"No, no. I want you in the room. I'll just stay on the floor."

"Uh. You sure? The couch is kind of nice and broken in and the floor is. . . well, hard."

"No, it's okay."

"Um... Do you want to talk or anything?"

"No. Just sleep. Please, Scott."

"Okay. I'm gonna go back to bed." Albeit concerned, I was vaguely annoyed, confused and tired. Long day. Crazy mother. Lack of father. "You can sleep where you like. Just let me know. I think there's blankets and stuff in the closet across from the bathroom."

"I'm sorry."

"Don't be sorry. I'm just tired."

"Okay. I just need to clean up. I'll be right in." She went into the bathroom and shut the door.

And so I went back into my room. She returned several minutes later with an armful of bedding.

"Anywhere on the floor?"

"Yeah. It's fine." She started spreading out sheets on the floor near my desk. Borrowed a blanket and a pillow from the end of my bed. It was kind of cute. Like making a nest.

When she was done, she sat on the bed next to me.

"You know, this is silly. Would you mind if I just shared?"

I put my book down. Uh.

"Uh."

"It's okay, it's just that now that I think about it, the floor isn't very comfortable." There is only one thing that is at the forefront of my mind and I try my hardest to be a neuter. "Elly, that's really not a good idea. My dad says my mom thinks we're, like, you know."

"But we're not, so it's okay."

"I think it would be better. . ."

"I'll explain to your mom in the morning if she's upset."

"I'm not even sure the assurance of Mother Teresa would make her feel better if she found out. She'll eat you alive and then kick me out. I'm already on her bad side..." I'm vaguely annoyed that she wants me in more trouble and feel like blaming someone. She isn't even asking me what's wrong.

"No, no, stay." She hopped next to me and pushed herself under the covers. Annoyance disappears and I suddenly became very aware of the fact that all this time I'd been without a shirt. I reached down on the floor to grab one.

"What?"

"I just. . .wanted to put this on." Over the head it went. Inside out. Tag on the front. But it was nice and not naked.

"Oh. Okay."

I turned out the light and slid to the other side of the bed. And then it was quiet. And I was wide awake.

God knows how long I sat there, staring into the dark.

But at some point, Elly moved closer and curled herself around my right arm. And then my chest. And I moved away. And she moved closer. And I was against the wall. And her arm was resting just under my chin. Had I shaved recently? Reminder to self not to move face.

It was at this point that air became a problem as well. If she was still awake, she could feel me breathing and I suddenly became very aware of my intake and outtake of oxygen. The space that my body took up suddenly became much too small for my own comfort and personal mental safety. I felt like screaming. Or not, since that would require a greater amount of breathing. And then maybe she'd think that I was out of shape. Because my respiration would be quicker than her own, so obviously I'd be out of shape. Or nervous. And of course I wasn't nervous. And even if I really was, she couldn't think so. Pretty girls slept in my *bed all the freaking time Jesus Christ I can't breathe.*

Until she kissed me. Breath control was not so much of a priority when that happened.

I'd like to think the kiss was more graceful than I could make it sound. So I don't think it's worth my trying. You get the idea, I guess.

Actually, maybe you don't.

"Elly, I love you."

Of course I can't just get away with losing my virginity. I have to trip on something or spill something or something has to come out of my nose. Or I have to tell someone I love them.

"Uh."

Something in my head told me that she simply didn't understand the words coming out of my mouth. I had to keep going. I was on a roll. In my head.

"Really, I mean it. I think I love you. You're perfect. You're everything—"

"Uh."

No, no, Scott, you're doing great man, keep going, she's eating this up, obviously. Just look at how she's backing out of your bed and searching for her bag.

"Elly, don't go. I just thought since..."

"I'm gonna head out."

She said this as she shut the door.

Fuck, dude.

Because I'm a crazy person, the only thing I could think to do was get in my mom's car and find her.

I found her at the grammar school playground.

And that brings us to page one.

THE SWINGS

"You didn't have to follow me. You're not even supposed to be driving."

"I'm sorry for what I said."

"Uh."

"It was really awkward and bad."

"Thanks. "

"No, no, I didn't mean that, I meant sort of...well...
like, you know."

"No, actually. Do you have a cigarette?"

"Yeah, in the car...I had half a one on the way over, but
I'm not sure about a match—you don't smoke, Elly."

"Fuck you."

"Uh."

"Not literally. Can you get me a cigarette?" She was
angry.

All tools, please report to your cars. I returned with
the half that I left in the ashtray and a booklet of Benni-
gan's matches that were in the glove box.

"Thanks." She took the cigarette from my hand and I
stood where I was to watch her light it. "Have a swing,
kiddo." She blew smoke in my face as she said this. And
so, I sat and watched her hold the cigarette close to her
lips. They were dry in the moonlight. God, they were
kind of gross. Were they like that before?

"I'm sorry, about the love thing."

"You don't even know about it."

"I just thought that maybe since, you know. . ." I nodded to indicate what I couldn't say. *YOU KISSED ME.*
Yeah, I couldn't say that.

"No. I just kind of...forgot who you were for a minute. That was stupid of me."

"Forgot? I'm right here. Remember me? I'm Scott!
Christ, Elly! How do you forget who I am?"

"Not forgot in that way."

"I'm not going to pretend I understand that."

"Maybe you will someday when you do something stupid."

She brushed her hair behind her ears. The t-shirt she was wearing looked enormous on her. Or maybe she was slowly shrinking into it. It was eating her alive. And her arms indicated a struggle. Oh man. Her arms.

"That wasn't stupid...I just...I dunno."

"Yeah, I don't either."

I had to ask: "Are you okay?"

"No worse than usual."

"I mean...like...are you *okay*."

More smoke in the face. "Can we, for once, not talk about it?"

"I just feel like we should talk about...*us*."

"You sound like a girl."

"Gee, thanks."

"Just forget about what happened, okay? Big fucking mistake, Scott. Got to clean up my act. I'll start with you, okay?"

"It wasn't! It wasn't! It wasn't a mistake, Elly. It was nice." Do it again! This time, with feeling!

"You don't love me."

"Elly. . ."

"You don't know anything about love."

"And you do?"

"More than just about anyone."

"Gimme a break." Between what she had just said and her dry lips, I suddenly became annoyed with her.

"I'll tell you who knows about love," she said.

"Who?" I said.

"Bono knows about love." Is how she replied.

A MILLION MILES UP

Like with all natural disasters that occur, I can tell you where I was when I got the phone call. Reading Roald Dahl. Still.

It was the day after the swings. Elly hadn't called. We both transgressed something, I guess. So I read all day. I didn't even feel like drinking. Not that I could have anyway. My mom had put a lock on the cabinet in the basement. I swear, no trust.

My mom made me an omelette when she got home from mass. She was distracted. Burned the first one. Stayed on the phone with various friends; priests. Cheating bastard. You wouldn't even believe where his car was parked. No. No, Scott is here. Wanted to slash his tires. Not since Friday. I left a note. Said I didn't want to see his face here for a very long time.

Bastard.

Bastard.

Bastard.

When she hung up the phone and put down my plate, she asked about my life. No mention was made of the morning before.

How is school? How are your friends? I told her about

the show I saw two weeks ago with Chris.

"You know, I haven't seen Chris around much lately. It was nice to see him the other week."

"Yeah. "

"So what did you two go and do?"

"City."

"For what?"

"Concert. "

"Who was it?"

"A band. Called Psychedelic Breakfast."

"Now there's a band name if I've ever heard one." Distracted smile. Thoughts elsewhere.

"Yeah. They were okay. More Chris's type of music."

"What kind was it?"

"Like jam-type music. The guitarist was absolutely ridiculous though. Really good. I do have to admit that."

"That's nice, hon. What're you reading?" She motioned to the book I had sitting upside-down and open on the table.

"*Switch Bitch.*" I kind of covered my mouth at my pronunciation of the word *bitch*.

"Who's that by?"

"Roald Dahl."

"Do I know him?"

"I dunno. He wrote, like, *The BFG* and stuff."

"Oh! Didn't you used to have that?"

"Yeah."

"Did he write *The Phantom Tollbooth*, too?"

"No."

"That was always one of your favorites."

"Yeah, it was. Good book."

"So this is good too?"

"Eh. Bunch of short stories. It's weird stuff. He was a weird guy."

"Good though?"

"Yeah. I picked it up on the book sale rack at the library."

"Can I take look at it when you're done?"

Take a look. Inspect. Watch. Watch. "I guess. I'll probably put it down on Dad's shelf." Dad. A slip of the tongue. I lower my head. Maybe she didn't notice.

She looks at me. "Okay. Let me know when you're through." Cold.

"I'm almost done. I'll probably be done by three."

"Are you going out with Chris again tonight?" In my mother's eyes, Chris was safe. Chris was responsible. Chris was a nice boy. Chris was still ten.

"No. Busy with Angela." Chris hadn't talked to me in the two weeks after he cheated on Angela with *my* Elly.

Well, more mine than his.

"Are you two okay?"

"I don't know. Maybe. Probably." Not.

"Okay. I'd hate to see a friendship like that go down the drain."

"Yeah. Me too."

"I'm going to go pick up Mallory's new kitten in about fifteen minutes. They're going away for the week, so we'll have some company." Another tired and unhappy raise of the corners of her mouth.

"Nice."

"Do you want to come?"

"No. I'll just stay here. I want to finish this."

"Okay." She got up and ruffled my hair.

"Right, mom." She hadn't heard a word we'd exchanged.

Silence. Omlette. Read. I was on the last short story and I was determined to finish it. When the phone rang.

And like I said, I can remember what I was doing. I was reading the following line: *And a moment later, the two of us were a million miles up in outer space.* What a way to describe a sex scene. And then, my mother called me.

"Scott... I think... You might want...to...uh...take this."

My mom wasn't going to pick up any kittens that day.

And I wasn't finishing any sex scenes.

And a moment later, the two of us were a million miles up...

CHRIST ON A HYPERCUBE

For those of you who have wondered what it would feel like to end up in a Dali painting, or a David Lynch film, I'll tell you.

Sunday, the day after Elly kissed me and I told her I loved her, she killed her dad. I'm not sure I should have seen it coming. I left the park before her. She told me she wanted to walk home. I felt like I'd done enough damage. So I let her.

Here is what everyone believed she did: After a long night out, Eleanor came home and sat in her new car at the top of the driveway, which was sloped. She listened to New Order until 7:30 a.m., when her father, Richard, came out of the house to get the Sunday paper. It was at that point that she put her car into neutral and it rolled down the hill, pinning him against the wall of the house.

The police said she had managed to practically sever his legs. He died on the way to the hospital. Blood loss? Internal injuries? I forget.

And what did Eleanor do? She sat in her car. Her mother came out. Called the police. Screamed her frail little head off. But Eleanor just sat there, listening to "Blue Monday". The police finally had to physically remove her from the car. Because as far as she was concerned, she wasn't going anywhere.

Her mother frantically called everyone she knew that Elly knew. Was Elly on drugs? Was Elly drinking? Did *your son* influence *my daughter* to do this?

Elly was sober. Elly was Elly. And God knew what that meant.

Elly left school. She wasn't there that much to begin with.

Elly was arrested. But then she wasn't anymore.

Elly moved somewhere. Far away, probably.

There was a trial. But Elly seemed to slip away from

that too.

Abuse. Physical? Definitely. Sexual? Both? Yes. Who knew! Maybe I should have.

And all this happened in no particular order.

Or maybe I just wrote it that way.

What did I do?

I called their house. A bunch. And Elly was never home. Of course not. She was on trial for homicide. Patricide? Or at least for a little while. 'Til they realized there was something wrong with her. She was broken. That's why she wanted to break him. Then they'd be even.

And in the end, all this made me wonder—am I broken, too? I feel different. Older. Tired. Much more tired. Or maybe I'm just seventeen.

All I knew was that I wanted to do what she wanted. Maybe, before, she wanted me to take her away. I failed at doing that if that was what she wanted. So if she wanted me to stay away now, I'd at least try and keep to that rule.

Did I do anything wrong? Maybe I should have mentioned the drinking...or the parties and the bathtubs and the master bedrooms and the cars. And the reading lamps. Maybe I should have talked her out of things, or protected her. Or maybe it would have happened anyway. Maybe I had nothing to do with it. Insignificant. What would make me think that what I did mattered?

Maybe because she made me feel like it did.

I had to go counseling, too. My parents. A real kind of counselor. Not like the counselor at school.

I told the counselor fantastic stories of my normality. Of my enthusiasm for life. And the nice woman behind the glasses very carefully nodded and noted. And sometimes, she'd ask questions, but never mentioned Elly unless I mentioned Elly. But I knew that Elly was the reason I was there. Somehow, she managed to fashion me in her image. And you can't come back from that sort of thing.

I don't think I'm really cut out to do much in the terms of normality, anyway.

I can pretend.

A little.

For now, I'm writing stories about a time-traveling stripper named Elly and her sidekick, Chip Butler. I am a well-adjusted social outcast. Aren't we all?

Break my heart.

Jennifer Davenport grew up in Wyckoff, New Jersey, outside of New York City. She graduated from Drew University where she majored in English. She works for a K - 12 school near her home in Nyack, New York, heading up their Technology Department. In her free time, she likes to travel, to eat good food, read and cycle. She can be found online at jenniferdavenport.net.